1

To: Shamaira

thank you for inspiring

the <u>MAGICK</u>!

WANDERLUST: An Autobiographical Fantasy

by Mary Ann Elizabeth

Illustrations by Cristina McAllister

i love you,

maemae

2

Copyright © 2011 by Mary Ann Elizabeth

ALL RIGHTS RESERVED

Printed in the U.S.A.

Tiger Press
155 Industrial Drive
Northampton, MA 01060
www.tigerpress.com

ISBN: 978-0-615-53286-8

Published by:
ALL ABOUT MAE
www.maryannelizabeth.com

Book Cover and Illustrations by:
Cristina McAllister
www.cristinamcallister.com
www.cristinasangels.com

ACKNLOWEDGEMENTS

I would like to thank the following contributors for their financial support on this project:

Matt and Lovecat Lovell, Jennifer Eightball, Stacey Pierce-Nickle, Samuel Harvey, Greg Young, Tiger Moon, Denise Scioli, Terry Helie, DivaDanielle White, Janet Barton, Alicia Talavera, Melissa, Tess Nagle, Diana Michaelangelo, Amy Boyer, Terri Robb, Emily Sinclair, Kylie Rickards, Dietmar Bloech, Robin Lamkie, Ruth Grayson, Lori Eicholzer, Laura Toy, Kari Tervo, Andie Villafane, Karl Partch, Gwen, Eva Lea, Marc Seymour, Karen Seymour, Laura Hippiechick, Evonne Heyning, Mark Zabala, Adam Erickson, Johnny Coy, Matthew Rogers, Marcus Ward, Lynn Drilling, Will Romano, Celeste Lear, Roby Duncan, John Halcyon Styn, Brainard Carey, Yehonatan Shai Koenig, Maria de Jesus Gutierrez, Mike Hawke, Julie Gross, Emily Goodwin, Suzanne Vasaeli, and Terry Helie.

A very special acknowledgement also goes out to Pamela Lane for all her support and for giving it to me straight.

4

<u>DEDICATION</u>

This book is dedicated to Black Rock City and to the legends who burn the man.

For DATIG, my beloved Nothing Fool muse, who inspired me to write this story.

5

FOREWORD

To say that the experience of writing this book has changed my life would be an understatement.

Once upon a time, now so very long ago, I was diagnosed with a mental disorder which, after much deliberation, was determined to be: anxiety-induced bipolar I with psychotic tendencies. The late and rapid onset of several traumatizing events in my life apparently triggered this madness and left me squandering for bits of sanity in a sick, twisted treatment program that included the kind of medication cocktail mixes that put psychiatry to shame.

In 2006, after being released from the kind care of people at Aurora Mental Institution, I chose to forego further drug treatment, a thought that alarmed my attending physician. His concern for my survival as a clinically insane person rested in staying medicated for the rest of my life. In defense of my position, I mentioned the fact that being on nine different medications certainly didn't dissuade my suicide attempt and I was interested in trying a different approach. Flabbergasted, he had no response.

It was then that I began my journey toward self-healing... a journey many would question, most of whom were loved ones with a very limited understanding of the struggle I faced. In 2007, I finally found a group of people who would best prepare me for the task at hand. They were, inevitably, a bunch of freedom-loving, brilliantly artistic, soulfully rich, and morally questionable people who showed me the fine art, nay... the FLAIR of how to fly my freak flag in the face of deceptively gusty societal zephyrs.

I've been esteemed to meet some of the most courageous, hard-working, talented, and yes – magical – souls I have ever known in my life from within this community. This book is a tribute to them and to the consciously-evolving community that is known as: BURNING MAN.

As a child, I was instructed to get my head out of the clouds, without any conception of just how wonderful it felt to soar through them on the back of a dragonfly nor the understanding that one can soar with their feet planted quite firmly on the ground. In the end, I've found that the key to sanity in an ever-increasingly insane world wasn't to be found in pills or shameful victimization, but instead waiting all along in the vast corners of my own imagination.

In conference with my last psychiatrist, she asked me what I planned to do – sans treatment – to secure my recovery. My reply was that somewhere along the way I stepped through the doorway of madness and was determined to find that door again, bringing the minds of many with me as we walked the safe passage of healing through the other side together. As you're about to witness, I found that door inside this very fantasy journey, along with the strength and style to not only walk, but waltz on through... keeping the doorway slightly ajar for our imaginations to wander at will.

We are not determined so much by the things that happen to us as by what we choose to do in light of them. I found the faith to not be afraid of the dark anymore. By virtue of doing so, I also had the pleasure of discovering the greatest magic of all... The sort of magic that's available to us all... Should we choose to open to it.

You are, hereby, cordially invited to become an "Alice" in a long line of Alices, with cherished child-like curiosity that will lead you on whatever particular creative endeavor tickles your fancy. You are also welcome here to join me in mine.

And so now, without any further ado... Open the doorway of your mind, waltz on through the other side, and dare to dream the impossible.

Mary Ann Elizabeth
2011

"Imagination is the door through which disease as well as healing enters."
¯Sri Yukteswar

PREFACE

"Never look back," the Caterpillar had advised, "Whatever you do." And yet, curiosity had gotten the better of her. So pulling a deep breath, she drew the door open once more and saw that there on the other side was... nothing. Nothing but a plain wall behind a very small door.

Many years later, once Alice had grown to become a woman, she would remember that land of magical wonders with fragile fondness in her heart. From time to time, she would tell the story to her only granddaughter as she tucked her in at night. Open doors and soft lights were an absolute must for her granddaughter while she slept, to avoid awakening in the midst of her all-too frequent night sweats.

No one knew precisely what caused these fears that ravaged the poor child so. This 'brain shock' with its chaotic circular logic, dramatic mood swings, nervous ticks, and ridiculous banter... Not even Grandma Alice could calm her at such times. The diagnosis from the doctors said there was something wrong with the girl, and while the evidence exactly of what the illness itself might be remained unclear, it was decided finally that it was an incurable sort of genetic snafu. Mary Ann's condition was considered an anomaly and often an unwanted subject at family functions. Constant reprimands were made, groundings for rebellious behavior issued, and medication administered to no avail.

There were times, for example, when the only words that came out of Mary Ann's mouth were rhymes and with a penchant for exaggeration, she also preferred using big words... an encyclopedia of which was catalogued from practiced reading of the dictionary. Grandma Alice encouraged her play with words, emphasizing the importance of calling a thing rightly. Any dinner squabble could be mitigated with a change in subject to a simple verb conjugation, impromptu spelling bee, or collaborative haiku whilst doing something as simple as passing the salt.

The family had come from France to join Grandma Alice in England during the latter part of the third trimester of her daughter's pregnancy. Mary Ann was born the seventh day after their arrival. It was suggested once that her birth was to blame for her parents' separation and mother's subsequent move cross Europe. The suggestion had been uttered only once.

The subject of Mary Ann's father was something never discussed within the family. He was more a mystery than anything.

Mary Ann's condition left her unable to leave the house for long periods at a time. Restricted to bed rest when the unnamed fever came roaring, it was difficult for the little girl to make friends. After awhile, she grew to accept the world from a distance... creating adventures inside her imagination while "normal" children made theirs outside on playgrounds and in parks. It was a life made simple on the outside that opened doorways to whole new, private worlds that no one but she visited.

Occasionally the outside world would collide with her private one, the result of which would tumult the very fabric of any given situation suddenly and without warning. This apparent disconnect from the outside world evolved into the ascension of secrets, imaginary friends, and a land of make-believe so profound that at times, Mary Ann felt as if her very life itself were being narrated in some grand Cosmic Storybook where plot ran thin in the vein of too many characters.

Grandma Alice's stories seemed the best remedy to soothe at evening time. It was a long-standing tradition the two of them shared, bedtime stories to usher in sweet dreams which would carry her through until morning. For how frightened the little girl would be to never catch a dream...

Alone...

In the dark.

9

PART ONE: A DREAM INSIDE A DREAM

whirly girl mine
whirly girl swirled
whirly girl wins
whirly girl world

CHAPTER ONE: LIGHTNING STORMS & MARCHING TOWERS

Mary Ann was an unusual child, given to spells. Whenever she raised a hand to her forehead, it was a sign of what she dramatically described as 'brain shock.' She absolutely swore to the death that at such times, every hair on her head could be felt with a certain degree of pain that tugged her brain in such a way that it felt inside out.

Lightning storms behind her eyelids was what she'd say. And when her nanny administered tablets to quiet her hurried mind, she'd toss them aside and lazily reply, "I simply want to crawl out of my skin and sink into a cup." When her nanny asked why, Mary Ann replied, "For some wise man to come and drink me up and know all the secrets of the universe."

"Silly girls with their wild imaginations," Mary Ann's mother would protest.

"Imagination, indeed!" answered Grandma Alice, never quite fond of her daughter's ever-so-practical ways. For she was, both Grandma Alice and Mary Ann decided secretly, an absolute bore of a person.

It was a bright sunny day when Mary Ann was released from the hospital. Too bright and too sunny, she secretly thought. It really would feel ever-so much more comforting if the sky would rain. The rain always comforted Mary Ann, for reasons she never exactly could explain.

When she returned home, she was met by her mother, nanny, and of course, her favorite person in the whole world – Grandma Alice, whom Mary Ann affectionately called 'Maemae.'

"Oh, good heavens!" cried her mother. "Well, just look at you, girl... You look simply dreadful! Let's get you into a bath and out of those filthy, unseemly clothes and into a pretty little dress that Mother bought for you while you were away."

"But I don't want to wear a dress! I like these patchwork pants and this fluffy tunic. It makes me feel quite smart."

"Indeed! You look like a ragamuffin! A hobo! Not a lady... A lady wears a dress. You want to be a lady, don't you, my darling?" her mother continued.

"I suppose not, if I must wear a silly dress to prove it," Mary Ann answered frankly.

Her mother, growing quite exasperated replied, "Enough of that, young lady! Up the stairs with you." Then to her nanny continued, "Make sure she gets behind the ears, do you hear?"

The nanny nodded and up the stairs they went.

Grandma Alice walked gingerly to her daughter and placing a delicate hand on her shoulder said, "I was far worse as a child and I wore dresses." Mary Ann's mother was not amused. Not in the slightest.

Grandma Alice just smiled her familiar half-turned smile and proceeded up the stairs to the bath, where she made certain the nanny had poured far, far more bubbles than were absolutely necessary.

After the long, luxurious bath, Grandma Alice brought forth her very loveliest of lotions and powders to cover Mary Ann up in, before slipping her into soft cotton pajamas.

"Oh Maemae Alice, how I do so love to smell just as sweet as you!" Mary Ann beamed. "Now I absolutely smell every bit as delicious as heaven."

Grandma Alice tucked her granddaughter snugly into bed. Having opened the window to let in a fresh breeze, she sat by the bedside in her wooden rocking chair.

"Shall I tell you a story, then?" she asked.

Mary Ann yawned, "Yes, I think you shall."

"Alright then," said Grandma Alice, "I wonder which story you would like most to hear."

"Maemae Alice, you know very well there's only one story to tell. But tell it all tonight... And no skipping bits. I want to hear every bitty detail, slowly and quietly, so I'll have to strain to hear. That way I'll stay awake until the very end."

"Oh, but my dear... Such a long day it's been for you. You really ought to get some sleep."

"I will sleep," Mary Ann said resolutely. "At the very end... and not a minute before!"

Grandma Alice brushed an amber strand of hair from her granddaughter's forehead, clearing a space for her to plant a soft kiss. "Very well, then... We shall start from the very beginning. With the white rabbit..."

And so she began, but it wasn't moments until Mary Ann drifted off to sleep soundly, clutching her ragged teddy bear.

Grandma Alice kissed Mary Ann's soft cheek, then turned down the bedside lamp, leaving it dimly lit. Through the flickering light she crept carefully out, leaving the door slightly ajar behind her.

CHAPTER TWO: THE MOCHAKIE CAT

    Mary Ann awoke with a start to the sound of thunder. Quickly looking to her right, she caught sight of rain pouring in her bedroom window. Running to the window and shutting it tight, she turned to find the strangest looking cat she ever had seen.

The cat was a good head taller and a great deal longer than any ordinary cat, with the kind of knowing grin that hinted suggestion of a secret never told a soul. Also, it sported an eye patch over its left eye and shoes on its feet, which was very odd, indeed, for a cat.

"Well, I say! WHO are YOU?"

And to her surprise, the cat answered, "I might ask you the same question."

"What crazy sort of dream IS this? With a talking cat!"

"Crazy, I should say assuredly so," replied the cat, matter-of-factly. "But dream on the other hand, I couldn't rightfully say at all."

"But how did you get in here?" asked Mary Ann. "The door is shut. Did you climb in through the window?"

"Firstly," began the cat, "Introductions, m'lady... If you please." Licking his paw to comb his whiskers, he continued with an air of great dignity, "I am Mochakie Cat."

"How'd you do?"

She reached her hand out in greeting.

Mochakie Cat rubbed pet whiskers against her paw.

She smoothed his fur in long, luxurious strokes from nose to tail.

"Cats have always been my very favorite of friends. I have a cat named Leoben. He's my only REAL friend."

Mochakie Cat jumped on the bed and curled up next to her.

"You know what they say about people with only one real friend..."

Mary Ann replied with some indignation, "I know, I know... I'm far too old to be playing with imaginary friends. Mother tells me all the time..." She sighed. "I suppose it doesn't fair me much better that the only real one I have is a cat."

Mochakie Cat purred, eyes closed in satisfied bliss, "People with only one real friend are quite obviously the single most purrrrfect friends to have!"

She gave the Mochakie Cat scritches under the chin. "It's not so hard to make friends. But to find a REAL friend... Well, that's not so easy at all. I wonder why it is that animals seem to be ever-so much easier to communicate with than people? Do you know?"

Mochakie Cat purred louder in reply.

Considering this lingering question, her thought brightened with another one. "How DID your fur not get soaked coming in from that downpour outside? Why, however DID you get in?"

"Curious are we?" Mochakie Cat grinned. "I can show you if you follow me. It's not far off... Just the teensiest hair of a walk." And with that, Mochakie Cat rose and gave his back a good stretch. He walked to the edge of the bed and continued prancing clear straight off... prancing on air, just as calm as can be.

'How DOES he do that?' thought Mary Ann, but instead said aloud as nonchalantly as possible, "So long as it's not far, I shall follow you to see. But that's only because I AM awfully curious... and my, how curiosity does make me often quite a bit peckish. Cat, do you mind if we stop for a bite from the pantry first?"

"No time," replied Mochakie Cat. "If you want to satisfy your curiosity, kitty cat, then your appetite must wait."

And with that, they were off... Out the door of her bedroom, down the hall, and through the front gate. Much to her surprise, the rain seemed to have stopped suddenly within the course of their sojourn. The grass underfoot not the least bit wet.

Mochakie Cat floating alongside a streetlamp called, "Well, are you coming or not?"

"I'm coming, cat!" said Mary Ann hazily, "I'm going as fast as I can! Perhaps if you swam through the air more slowly, I could more easily keep up."

Mochakie Cat stopped, tapping his tail mid-air. Once she had caught up to him, he floated off again and paused in front of a house that Mary Ann didn't remember ever having seen before.

"Is this house quite new? Has it been built since I left for that dreadful hospital?"

"Sometimes..." answered Mochakie Cat, "We can walk by quite obvious things everyday and never notice them at all." And with that, he floated straight through the front door, opening it as he went.

The poor girl was caught in an eerie sort of trance, her gaze mesmerized by the fantastically seussian abode, complete with a weather vane perched high in the shape of the Mochakie Cat himself. Curiouser and curiouser...

Mary Ann followed nervously. Into a foyer of doors, she tiptoed. It was a very odd foyer, circular in shape, with a round wood table in the center. On the tabletop, leaning off-kilter rested a small porcelain vase with a single red rose nesting safely inside. Surrounding her on all sides, were a series of doors of various shapes and sizes.

She looked about for the cat, but he was gone... Could he be behind one of those doors?

As she inspected each of them, she found every door locked, save one which stood slightly ajar... A flickering light invitingly beckoning from beyond.

"Without a key, I suppose I have no choice but to take the opened door," she reasoned aloud. And with a trepidatious hand, she nudged it further wide and stepped through.

It was a dark room, which made it difficult to see. But there in a not too distant shadow sat Mochakie Cat on the brim of a reclining chair.

"Well, where are we now, cat? Whose house have you led me into? And why is it so dark in here? I absolutely cannot STAND the dark."

"How should I know whose house we're in..." answered the Mochakie Cat. "You chose the door, not me."

"But it was the only one open!"

"Yes well. You might have looked for a key like Alice," Mochakie Cat said smugly.

"I shan't know where I might have found such a key."

"It takes some doing for an Alice to discover, my dear..."

Mary Ann pouted. "Now listen here! My name isn't 'Alice.' It's –" Her voicing trailing off, wondering what in heaven's name this cat could know about her grandmother and thinking in the process that it was rather strange how there'd been a cat in the story she'd told, too.

Getting back to tack, Mary Ann twirled a strand of hair between her fingers (a sure sign she was thinking) and continued, "Do well to remember this is MY dream you're in! And being such, I shall charge you with the command of giving me some semblance of direction." She added tartly, "Please."

"Ah, I see! YOUR dream, is it? Seems you ought to direction yourself, then... If it is so. And if it isn't, why then... Who am I to say? I'm just a cat, remember?"

"You might know some direction if you were a smart cat," she teased.

To that, Mochakie Cat didn't bother with a reply. His tail swatting this way and that.

"I say," she finally continued, "The only way to know if you're a smart cat or not is for you to tell me which way to go from here."

Flick-flick went the tail smartly.

"Which way do you want to go?"

"How should I know?"

"How should you, indeed," remarked Mochakie Cat with a snarky purr, "Whichever way you should go is the way that you choose and the way that you choose is something only an Alice could say."

"I do so wish you'd stop calling me Alice," she said then, "My name is Mary Ann!"

Mochakie Cat purred, "I shall remember from now on, I purrrromise," crossing his paw across his heart. "As should you do well to remember, too."

"Silly cat, why ever would I forget my own name?

"You'd be surprised..." And with that, Mochakie Cat vanished into thin air with an all-too familiar grin.

CHAPTER THREE: DREAMNESIA

Mary Ann, now greatly perplexed, decided that resting in the reclining chair was the best way to collect her thoughts. This was all so strange; somehow familiar yet strange, and she really had no idea what to think of the cat, or the foyer of doors, or this house that she'd never seen before on her street.

She sat and wondered... then wondered some more... and soon all that wondering had her wondering till bored. She decided next that a nap was in store, so she pulled on the lever to the right of the chair for more comfortable angle in the seat there. Settled herself in and leaned back for a spell, then presently into a deep sleep she fell.

A deeper sleep than Mary Ann had ever fallen before. Downward and downward, she felt herself falling... Deeper and deeper... Darkly downward as if the weight of her eyelids was shutting her in.

When she awoke suddenly to the start of a sneeze, her brain felt quite twitchy. She sprang to her feet, startled to attention.

The chair, still comfy, still reclined, and still sound... was positioned in a thicket surrounded by things that she'd lost now there found. There was the stuffed bunny she loved... lost in kindergarten, a white glove thought stolen from a church gathering donut sale, a teacup (her favorite) she'd assumed her dollies had hidden, and most especially of all, an old tattered notebook she'd written her first stories in.

"My goodness gracious, whatever IS this place?" asked Mary Ann brightly. "It seems to be wonderful, whatever it is, to have given me back all my treasures I'd cried so over for missing."

"You've missed them, have you?" asked a voice from nowhere in particular. "We might say the same for you!" Then out from behind a gnarled tree, hopped a rat with a hat.

"I say, what's this? And how could you miss me very much if I don't even know who you are?"

"Know me? HA!" cried the rat. "Fun and games, wasn't it always, Alice?" and with a flamboyant curtsy of the hat, the rat transformed into a witch... a long-haired, snaggle-toothed witch with a mole the size of a one pence on the side of her crooked nose. "We know each other well, my child. You might not remember, but that's another thing entirely. All things in good time... You'll remember soon enough."

'Remember soon enough,' thought Mary Ann to herself. Then she said aloud, "Why must everyone address me as if I don't remember anything?"

"Having a hard time, are we?" queried the Good Witch with a smile. "Is it the remembering that's catching you up or the catching up that's making it hard to remember?" She waited for a reply, then continued, "I see. Both then. There is someone you should meet who will help you with this remembering business. One word of warning, however... You mustn't be scared of him. Wolf absolutely hates it when little girls are scared of him. He finds it... Trite."

"A wolf? Well, who wouldn't be scared of a wolf?" asked Mary Ann.

"Me, for one," answered a voice from behind. And there, as she turned, stood a wolf reclining against the trunk of a tree, picking his teeth.

Mary Ann jumped back a foot, startled beyond belief.

"Oh come now, child. You act as if you've seen a ghost. I'm no ghost. I'm altogether real, silly. But I do sooooo like silly, so silly on as you please."

"But it's quite difficult to be silly when facing such foreboding fangs," Mary Ann admitted. "It's the teeth that frighten, I should say, not you entirely Wolf, but the teeth."

Then from the tree above Mary Ann's head, came a wooing sound that swept through the wind, like the ghost perhaps that the wolf had warned her about.

"Whoooooo... Whoooooo..... Whooooooooooo are yooooooooooou?" said the wind.

"I shan't know which to be more afraid of," said Mary Ann unknowingly out loud, "The Wolf or this ghost now."

"Haaaa haa haaa!" laughed the Wolf, now showing his sharp teeth. "That's no ghost, my girl. That's just good ol' Owl up the tree!"

Mary Ann looked up and there, indeed, in the tree on a branch far above the Wolf sat a rotund Owl perched precariously on a broken tree limb.

Wolf removed his hat with a chivalrous grin, "My name is Wolf... Easy enough to remember, eh? Anything coming back to you yet, then?"

"What? No. Not yet, I guess."

"Ah, then. We shall wait until morning and see what fresh dawn brings to your stuffy little head," said the Wolf.

Mary Ann looked about, glancing at the sunlight dripping off the morning dew of the grass all about. "But is it not morning already?" she asked, quite confused.

"So it IS! So it is," said Wolf. "Glad to see you're at least paying attention. Good. That's very, very good!"

She shuddered from his disguised reproach. "It's those teeth, I tell you... They make you look mean."

Wolf nodded for Mary Ann to come closer. She did so cautiously.

He nodded for her to come closer still, as if about to whisper a secret in her ear. She turned her ear towards him, eyes fixated on his dripping fangs.

"This showy display of teeth is nothing more than a put on, my girl," he said then, adding with a shrug, "Inside I'm actually as sweet as a bunny rabbit."

Mary Ann glanced at the lost and found artifacts nestled round the reclining chair. The stuffed bunny rabbit caught her eye, shook his head voraciously, then hopped away into the forest.

She did not take this as an encouraging sign. Unsure whether or not Wolf was jesting, she considered her lessons from home. 'A good show usually accompanies a fib, even if the fib is hidden inside a joke' she thoughtfully recalled. And since presently the Wolf had gone absent-mindedly back to picking his teeth without any sense of decorum whatsoever, the innocent child remained unclear as to the intention of the Wolf's secret.

"Why, bunny rabbits have big teeth too, as they've also been known to bite!" she countered, searching for a clue.

Wolf laughed. "Of course! But why would anyone be frightened of a bunny? Now that's VERY silly, indeed! Well done, Alice... Excellent use of silliness! I must say... BRAVO!"

"Well, thank you very much for your approval but I don't see how all this is helping me much with my lapsed memory."

"Never mind that," spoke the Good Witch with a swish of her hat, turning it upside down instantly into a wine goblet which she took a deep drink from. "All things in good time. All things in good time."

CHAPTER FOUR: THE LAND OF LOST TOYS

"Fetch me my slippers and my hat, Alice. My slippers and hat!" cried Wolf.

"But my name isn't Alice!" said Mary Ann quite defiantly. "Why must people keep calling me something I am not?"

"Oh come now, child. A name isn't something you are, unless you want it to be. And I MUST refuse you calling me a person... A person is something that walks about on two feet. A quite unsteady creature."

'It's true,' thought Mary Ann. 'Wolf does walk quite surely, thought he tends to use his legs mostly for resting.'

"My gloves and hat, if you please!" Wolf repeated.

'Well now, that's odd... I could've sworn he'd said SLIPPERS and hat not more than a moment ago...' the poor child thought, 'Perhaps my remembering is still a bit fuzzy. Either that, or my ears have cotton fluff inside.'

She bustled about for the hat, but there were neither gloves nor slippers to be found anywhere.

"Hat! Hat! Hat!" Wolf decreed, growing impatient.

Hurriedly, Mary Ann snatched her own pair of white gloves from the lost and found stack. She carefully folded them inside his hat.

Fearing fangful reproach, she approached cautiously, handing Wolf the hat. Upon fitting the gloves on his paws, he found them (obviously) much too small. So he plucked a pair of scissors from his pocket and snipped the ends off of each glove's finger. Once delicate little lady gloves, they now seemed hoboish, but fit him right as rain never-the-less.

"W-what shall we d-d-d-do t-t-today for adventure?" started Owl.

"You must excuse Owl," explained Wolf. "He's given to bouts of stammering, caused undoubtedly by his fretful condition."

"Oh dear! What condition is that?"

Wolf shrugged. "Fairly decent mostly, however prone to anxiety-induced insomnia."

"I s-s-s-sleep f-f-fine," defended Owl to himself. "I j-j-just l-like to s-s-s-sleep with my eyes open m-m-most of the t-time."

Mary Ann spoke towards the branch above then, "To your point, Owl... Sleep or resting eyes for whatever matter I don't much see the point in arguing. However, as for adventure, I shan't know what options we have here in this place, seeing as I've just arrived and all... Do you have any good suggestions?"

"F-fairly d-d-decent ones m-mostly," was his reply.

"Well then? Let's hear your ideas, then... No use telling someone you have fairly decent ideas if you're not going to mention what they ARE." She exhaled audibly in frustration. "Honestly!"

"Speaking of which, I think I've honestly lost my marbles most completely this time..." the Good Witch began.

"Whatever did you lose this time, my darling?" asked Wolf, snapping a final stitch in the waistcoat he'd been sewing.

"My marbles. I am forever losing my marbles!" She bobbled her head as if shaking water out her ear. "They must be 'round here somewhere..."

Admiring the handiwork on his fancy waistcoat, Wolf offered, "You might want to look inside your pouch, love."

By now the Good Witch was in quite a tizzy, peering in every which direction at frenzied pace... Under even the most impossibly small pebble, inside every overgrown mulberry bush... Her frantic searching paused for the briefest of moments.

"Pouch?"

Wolf tied off the stitch and tried on the waistcoat.

"Yes, Good Witch... The marble pouch."

He turned then to Mary Ann, standing quite tall and proud... hands in both lapels, showing off his craftiness.

"Well, what do you think?" Wolf asked.

Mary Ann took a good gander, eyeing Wolf scrupulously up and down before nodding.

"Not bad at all... For a Wolf, that is."

Wolf snarled lowly.

"Oh, I found them! I found them! My marbles are found, safe and sound!" she shrieked. Then to Mary Ann continued, "You know, you really ought to apologize. Wolf made that waistcoat all on his own." Then to Wolf, "And it looks dashing! Excellent work, friend."

Wolf straightened again, proudly.

"Thank you. I thought it quite smart, myself..." he touted.

"W-w-w-wonderf-f-fully s-s-smart ind-d-deed," Owl offered.

Mary Ann cowered, "I'm awfully sorry to have hurt your feelings, Wolf. You do look quite smart. It's just that I've never had to make any clothes myself, you see... so I really haven't the foggiest notion of how to configure something by design."

Wolf picked a piece of lint from Mary Ann's sleeve.

"I really have no idea what HAVING to make clothes has to do with anything... Why, how much fun would things be if all we ever did was what we HAD to do? That doesn't seem anywhere near silly." He eyed her scrupulously then added, "I liked you better when you were on the silly tack."

"Enough squabbling over silly things!" the Good Witch ordered. "I have an idea for adventure for us all and it happens to involve the hand-making of costumes."

Owl clapped his wings together in anticipation. "Oh g-g-goody! W-w-w-where sh-sh-shall we g-g-g-go?"

"I believe the Land of Lost Toys is a good place to start," spoke the Good Witch. "Wolf, would you be kind enough to help us with our costumes, my good man?"

Wolf bowed with the grandest of gestures, tipping his hat to the Good Witch then Mary Ann. "Ladies... It would be my honor."

After some debate as to which particular costume would be the best fit for Mary Ann, the Good Witch dragged forth from the belly of her hat, a large sewing machine.

"Let's get started then, shall we?"

Mary Ann loved to play dress up. Halloween had always been her favorite holiday for that very reason. So the thought of going to a costume ball was simply almost too much for her short patience to bear.

Entering the masquerade hall with Wolf, Owl, and the Good Witch, Mary Ann smiled from ear to ear, marveling at the Shiny! Shiny! all around.

The masquerade hall was ensconced in silvery blue gleam with strobing lights flashing from each of the four corners of the room. Ornaments hung brightly from table lamps and a curious looking-glass on the far wall, which shone a non-reversed reflection.

Wolf made the formal introductions. "Alice, this is so-and-so" and so on and so forth. To her surprise, each and every dressed-up toy she met hugged her in greeting, which felt ever-so much more friendly than the stuffed shirt handshakes she received back home. 'Mother would assuredly hate this place,' thought Mary Ann, which made her love it all the more.

Wolf introduced her to someone who looked very familiar indeed to the little girl. She did, in fact, look quite exactly (aside from the costume obviously) like Mary Ann's nanny back home. 'That's awfully strange,' thought Mary Ann to herself. 'What would my nanny be doing HERE, I wonder?' The thought then crossed her mind that perhaps the nanny was sent here to make certain that she mind her manners and take her medicine as instructed. This thought disturbed her so that she took extra care in remembering this woman so that she could avoid her whenever and as much as possible.

The nanny-looking woman was named Lala, which Mary Ann considered thoughtfully would be easy enough to recall since her best friend was named Sophia Farfalla... And Lala sounded ever a lot similar. She must simply keep straight, however, that Sophia FarFALLA was someone she quite liked and that this Lala nanny-impersonator was the LA to be avoided.

Oh, how she dreaded taking that horrible medicine. Every night before her bath, the nanny would pull a bottle out of the cabinet and often struggle so as to pin Mary Ann down to get it all in. She found it really was quite hard to swallow how her mother could believe the doctor when he told her that without it Mary Ann wouldn't survive. The obviousness of this lie made Mary Ann hate not only the medicine, but also her mother for believing in the doctor's word over her own.

Lala approached Mary Ann exclaiming, "Why, don't you just look darling! - A real live doll!"

"I'm not a doll," retorted Mary Ann emphatically. "I'm just dressed up like one, that's all. Wolf dressed me up like this. I had wanted to go as a yo-yo."

Lala laughed. "But however would you have dressed up as a yo-yo? It's a darling idea, but a doll is so much cuter for your darling little frame. It really does suit you so."

"I suppose that's why Wolf chose to go with the doll idea then," replied Mary Ann, feeling stodgy.

"Well, it's simply adorable anyway. You really are SUCH a darling little girl!"

Mary Ann's head whirled. Too many darlings came out of that woman's mouth and it made her mind flip flop to the nanny shoving those awful tablets down her throat.

Suddenly, the columns on the dance floor morphed into those dreaded marching towers that stored all that nasty medicine that made her mind itch. The room swirled with confusion. The towers approaching steadily, ready to attack. Mary Ann could take the fright no further and fell with a THUD! to the floor.

When she came to, it was the face of the Good Witch Mary Ann first saw, hovering above her.

"Everybody step back. Give her some room to breathe!"

"Oh f-f-for heavens to b-b-betsy... I d-d-d-do so hope she's alright!" added Owl.

The Good Witch soothed gently the little girl's sweaty brow with a sweet pet of her steady hand. "Not so fast, little one. You've had a tough spill. What is it that you need?"

Mary Ann's head buzzed with the thought of marching towers, her nanny, her mother, and those horrible doctors who scolded and lied. She thought of all those wicked nightmares and the lightning storms behind her eyelids. She thought of that terrible wretched brain shock... and in consideration of all these things, she answered the Good Witch simply with the word: "Peace."

"Piece of what, my sweet?" queried the Good Witch softly.

"Peace. Just peace. A bit of peace of mind," Mary Ann began and with that, she fell unconscious again.

"Oh n-n-n-n-nooooooo!" howled Owl.

"Did she say she wanted pie? A piece of pie?" asked Wolf.

"Peace of mind is what the poor child seeks," the Good Witch replied with a nod. Then pushing back her sleeves, she spread her arms open wide over Mary Ann's quite raggedy doll body lying limp on the floor and pronounced loudly:

"A la kazoo
A la kazam
Bring this child
Tatatamtam

Silk of the air
Always enough
Cover these eyes
In wings of a love"

And with that, Mary Ann opened her eyes suddenly.

"W-w-w-wings of a love?" wooed Owl from above.

"Dove, you silly hoot. Wings of a dove. Not pie or love does this girl seek, but peace of mind," corrected the Good Witch.

Wolf produced a flowerful butterfly kerchief from his breast pocket, which he used in hand to lift Mary Ann to her feet.

"You did say 'love', Witch. It was 'love' that you spelled," said Wolf, steadying Mary Ann with his arm.

"I didn't!" The Good Witch drew a stunned breath adding, "Or did I?"

Owl hooted affirmatively.

"Oh dear," said the Good Witch gravely. "Then this child shall know no peace of mind presently, indeed."

"Clumsy witch, you put her under the wrong spell," quoth an ugly Troll from beside her. And with a thrust of his cane forward, offered Mary Ann a chair to sit.

"How very kind of you, sir," said Mary Ann queasily.

"Oh... My pleasure, sweet lady," the Troll cooed then kissed her delicate hand. With that kiss sealing the Good Witch's misspell.

Despite her better judgment, Mary Ann was ushered out of from the masquerade of the Land of Lost Toys with the Troll. So swept up in the excitement of this new friend that she remembered quite after the fact that she'd left all her true ones behind.

CHAPTER FIVE: MERRY BAND OF THIEVES

"Oh... You're so pretty, m'lady! So very pretty, indeed! I like your dress, m'lady... It's very proper. How proud it feels to have you as m'lady!"

'How he DOES blather on...' thought Mary Ann to herself. 'I rather wish he'd give it a good rest.'

"So, have you thought about what you'd like to do together? Cuz I was thinking of a whole lot of exceedingly fun things to do together... Like climbing trees, or skipping rocks, or --"

Mary Ann interrupted then, "I hate to be rude, but I've had a terrible spill and my headache surely isn't going to be cured with your incessant prattling on!"

"Oh... Am I talking too much, is that it? Are you mad at me, then? Are you, m'lady? Are you quite mad?"

"I'm not mad, Troll. I just have a headache."

"Oh... I understand, m'lady... I do. It's just that I want us to be fast friends is all and you seem so awfully quiet. I thought to pass the awkward space with some conversation while we walk is all. Just conversation." He pounded his fuzzy knuckle on his head. "There I go again... prattling! Prattle, prattle, prattle!"

"Now listen here, Troll... I'm not sure where it is that you've taken me, but MY FRIENDS are back THERE at the Lost Toys ball. Do you remember the way we came so I can find them again?"

"Oh... No, m'lady. I don't know that I could and even if I could, I'm not certain that I would since well... You're very pretty, indeed, m'lady!"

Mary Ann stiffened in disgust.

"Why, you impudent ogre! So you think you can steal me away with flattery, is that it?"

"Oh... But m'lady! It's not flattery if it's the truth! And empirically speaking, you ARE Very Pretty!"

"Once and for all, I'm not YOUR lady! I'm not a LADY at all... at least that's what Mother always says. There's no point in calling me things I'm quite obviously not."

The Troll dropped his head, definitely dismayed.

"Oh... well. But you are still pretty," he offered cowering in fear for her reply.

"If you can't help me find the way back and you've nothing else to say besides this 'pretty' nonsense then I'd ask again that you do shut up."

This hurt the Troll's feelings greatly, but because he wanted to make her happy, he did just as she commanded and didn't say another word about her prettiness or things to do or anything else.

Along a wiry little patch of wood, Mary Ann and the Troll came, quite unexpectedly, upon a loaded gun... Spot in the face, if you please. Behind the other end of the barrel of that rifle stood the most fantastically clad beard Mary Ann had ever laid eyes on.

"Don't mind us... Just mozyin' on through here, folks... And we thought we'd relieve you kind folk of any precious artifacts you'd wish to impart on us," said the Beard.

"But we ARE precious artifacts, sir. Do you propose we relieve ourselves, then?" queried Mary Ann, matter-of-factly.

After a longer than anticipated moment of possibly jarring yet none-the-less admirable pause, the Beard declared, "You may stay."

And with a swoosh of his rifle into the face of the Troll, the Beard further professed, "You I'm not so sure about, but the little one can stay."

Mary Ann objected, "Oh no, sir. I know he looks quite hideous and his odor is somewhat alarming, but I assure you this Troll is nothing short of harmless. Or at least, when he isn't blathering on and on. Though, come to think of it, I couldn't rightfully say whether he is exactly harmless or not for we ourselves have only just met. But seeing as we are traveling companions for the time being, I would appreciate it if you'd lower your pointed gun. It does seem to be upsetting him ever-so."

She was right. The Troll's face contorted into a twist of shocked fear brazened into the creases of his furrowed brows.

'A most appalling display on ungallantry!' thought Mary Ann, with an overly nonchalant expression washing over her face.

The Beard cautiously sized up the Troll, glancing back at Mary Ann for confirmation of what he inwardly thought to be nothing short of a coward. The rifle was holstered carefully and immediately following, the two of them were wrapped up in hugs from every side. Squeezed so, Mary Ann thought she might falter (after the spill she'd just had, it had been quite a challenge to regain a sense of steadiness, you know) but falter she did not.

Not knowing for absolute certain if these strange characters were themselves harmless, she kept her guard up, which in the end was altogether helpful in maintaining her balance – and her posture – from falling to the ground.

"I'm Barak," quoth the Beard.

Mary Ann's eyes scanned the scene. "And this must be your Merry Band of Thieves," she added finally after thoughtful pause.

Barak laughed. "Oh, that's good... I like it!" Then he caught himself in rocky stance and stumbling a tad continued, "Would you like a nip of scotch? It is a might cold out... Prolly keep ya goin', no doubt. Wind's blowin' up a gale from the north. Have you been up north, by the way? Beautiful country... Hear it's chilly though... Course it's chilly here, too... But I already mentioned that. Wind makes fer chillier temperatures though... Chill to the bone kinda cold, if ya catch my drift." Then pausing curiously to look carefully at Mary Ann, the Beard continued, "Say, have we met before? Your face seems awfully familiar."

"Awfully sorry," said Mary Ann.

Bearded Barak shook his head. "So strange... Feels like our paths have crossed before... Did we catch your name already?"

"I'm Mary Ann," she said then, offering her hand in greeting. "How'd you do?"

Barak nodded approvingly as he vigorously shook her tiny hand. "Well, as mentioned, I'm Cap'n Barak" then pointing with a gesture of grand presentation to a cute pixie woman to his right added, "And this here's my gal Jag."

Mary Ann curtseyed in greeting.

"Pleasure to meet you all."

"We haven't actually met," said a red-headed stranger next to her, extending his hand. "Steve," said the cheery face. Then placing his arm around a bodacious blonde beside him continued, "And this is Daisy. Daisy Red Rider."

"A-ha!" cried the Troll finally speaking, directing his aim at Daisy. "Oh... We've already got a wolf and now the red rider! Might that wolf be the same one who gobbled you up whole? Did he spit you out, then? Must have been terribly difficult to digest all of that pretty... bosom. Or was it perhaps another wolf? There can't be two wolves, you know. A story with two wolves will never do."

Mary Ann turned quickly, facing the Troll. "Who's to say if one or two wolves WOULD do, Troll? Last time I checked this wasn't YOUR story to rightfully say."

Then thinking to herself that she quite liked it better when the Troll held his tongue, added to Steve, "I'm ever-so sorry for my companion's impudence. He simply has the manners of a goat."

"Yes well, I'm not Red Riding Hood, silly," answered Daisy smiling. "That's a different story altogether."

"Do you ride in a red truck, then?" Mary Ann asked curiously.

"Daisy IS the ride!" answered Steve with the cheery face. Steve and Daisy apparently found this last bit VERY funny, what with giggles tickling back and forth between them.

"Well, that makes sense!" replied Mary Ann, though she really hadn't the foggiest idea why they were laughing,

Cap'n Beard Barak clapped his hands together loudly. "Well well, that's it then! Off we go!" And with that, the Merry Band of Thieves followed him through a thicketed patch of forest that looked very much like an untrail-like trail.

The Troll glanced briefly at Mary Ann, shrugged, and then followed suit behind the others.

"But where are we going?" called Mary Ann after them.

"Why, haven't you seen the sign?" Cap'n Beard Barak called back.

"What sign?" she yelled in reply.

The pixie gal Jag stopped in her tracks, turned to face the little girl then pointed to the night sky. "Look UP!"

And there, high up in the trees, clear as day, was a giant glowing arrow with the words "MYSTERY FUNLAND... DON'T MISS IT!" shining right above where she stood. The arrow pointing, of course, exactly in the direction to which they were headed.

CHAPTER SIX: THAT CAMP & STUFF N THINGS

Lounging around the fireplace of That Camp (formerly known as MYSTERY FUNLAND... DON'T MISS IT!) Mary Ann was introduced to two new faces. The first was a Fool for he seemed given to the telling of bad jokes and querying riddles. Next to him, seated on the ground smoking a pipe, was the darkest man whom Mary Ann had ever laid eyes on. The dark man was called Shaman Ka and the Fool accompanied him in this one of his many travels.

Story told that the Shaman Ka seemed to flow through disciples faster than a tortoise could outrun a hare, and as effectively, too. First it was a mathematician named Lajik he tried teaching magic to, but Lajik just came up with equations that the Shaman couldn't compute. He gypsyed on from there, declaring that intuition alone was the key to a treasure chest that consciousness couldn't open.

He then met a wordsmith named Rashun A. Liddy whom he tried to convert to the path of truth, but far too many words spoken by Rashun were far too trite for the Shaman to properly translate. He said again that intuition alone was the key to a treasure chest that consciousness couldn't open.

Then the Shaman Ka happened one day upon the Fool who had nothing much at all to say except "Do All Things In Goodness" and "Have A Nice Day." The Shaman Ka traveled alongside the Fool for awhile, humbly becoming his follower. He learned a great deal of absurdity which served to illuminate his awareness in the way that only a thing like absurdity can. Not long afterwards (so the story goes), the deep magic of the Shaman Ka grew so powerful that he had to move far, far away from everyone he had ever known. At this very moment, however, Mary Ann happened upon them in that in-between period where the two of them were quite joined at the hip. She found it striking that seated together, the Shaman Ka and the Fool looked just as different as night and day yet somehow seemed to fit together like pieces of a puzzle long forgotten.

Speaking of forgotten, it suddenly occurred to Mary Ann that the Troll was nowhere to be seen and she hadn't the slightest remembrance of when she'd last seen him. Having given a moment to pause in consideration of where he might have sneaked off to (and secretly wondering guiltily that she might have scared him away), she decided almost as quickly as the thought popped into existence that she didn't care enough to bother looking for him.

'I never much liked that Troll anyway,' she thought. 'He gave me the absolute willies.' Then with a shivering smile she added aloud, "Good Riddance" and didn't give the Troll another thought, except in fleeting regret that he'd led her away from her faithful friends at the Land of Lost Toys.

If there was to be a place where she might feel comforted to be so lost in this land that made no sense at all, the warm hut of That Camp was it. Inside was featured the most elaborate crystal chandelier and dainty sun-catchers dangling all about from the thatched ceiling above. Where the sun-catchers gathered their light was a conundrum to Mary Ann, for not much light pours forth from the night sky. She noticed curiously that the dangling crystals seemed to shimmer rainbows from floor to wall each time the pixie gal Jag strolled in and out, offering treats and tea in tow.

Wiping a swig of scotch from the brow of his beard, Cap'n Beard Barak regaled tale after tale to rapt audience, gathered 'round in a semi-circle before him. Until finally, spilling over onto the floor, laughing merrily, the gang raised a toast and cheerfully sang:

"Barak Barak the party king
Does whatever a party king should
Flexes his muscles
Make the pretty girls sigh
Pour you a drink
Get you rightly high

His stories are great
His feather is long
Catch him in a dream
You'll fetch a catchy song

Holds you in a hug
You'll be holding back from time
Heart deeper than his pocket
Trade ten dozen for a dime

His eyes possess a siren call
He hides behind his shades
Keeping safe from falling fast
Protects his fair shore maids

The King is good
The King is strong
The King has all his people
Gathered 'round most every night
To worship at his steeple"

Then with a sloshing CLINK! of glasses, a resounding "Cheers!" and hearty "Here, here!" was heard before more regaling resumed.

The sweet treats they fed Mary Ann made her tummy feel full, followed by tangy confections to make the up seem inside out. Following that, came curiously strong mints to freshen and smooth the inside out feeling.

Too many sweets, or could it be the confections or the mints, perhaps? All of a sudden, Mary Ann felt altogether strange. The grandfather clock to the left of the fireplace mantle melted slightly onto the floor, forming a puddle where an octopus floated and with one tentacle waved ominously.

Mary Ann looked around the room, her eyes landing on her reflection in a looking-glass just above the fireplace. Standing beside her, perched lackadaisically against an upright (albeit broken) piano, the reflection of the Fool there bore such a striking resemblance to the Hatter heard tale of many times by Maemae Alice in her bed-time story.

The Nothing Fool waxed philosophy nonsensically, riddling on in his jesterly way and Mary Ann was ever-so much enjoying his company and conversation, when on second glimpse of their reflection in the looking-glass hanging now quite off-kilter, her attention was turned. As the Fool tattled on, her gaze was caught in a most curious sight, indeed! For there inside the looking-glass, she looked quite a lot not like herself at all.

The reflection of the Hatter Fool turned toward her with whirly twirly eyes gone mad and said quite profoundly, "Well, hello again, Alice!" Before she could get a peep out (for the words wouldn't seem to come) he continued, "I've been waiting for you for ages, my sweet. Tea just hasn't been the same without you. But I say, Alice... You look better than ever! Just smashing, I say... Smashing!"

Mary Ann shook her head in confusion, tears of fear she was too embarrassed to explain pouring down her face.

The Hatter Fool with the whirly twirly eyes queried, "Why, Alice, why? Why tears, my dear?"

But before she could form the words to complete her thought, her reflection morphed into Maemae Alice herself, wearing Mary Ann's very own Raggedy Ann costume that Wolf had helped design for the Land of Lost Toys masquerade ball.

Maemae Alice's reflection spoke then. "I knew you would make it!" whereupon Mary Ann, bewildered beyond belief, hid her face in her hands and sobbed.

To the mocking whirly twirly eyes she exclaimed, "I shan't know why a raven is like a writing desk, Hatter... and I am not your Alice. I am not!" Then heaving a giant sigh, "I am nothing."

The Fool, upon catching his new friend talking to her reflection in the looking-glass, suggested they play a game together to get her mind unstuffed.

"Looking too long at a thing sometimes makes stuff hard to see clearly. I should know... I happen to be an expert at Stuff N Things!" the Fool said with great confidence.

Mary Ann felt her mouth form the words, "Yes, but..." The rest of the sentence took a moment of determined effort to finish. "But... I'm not much for games."

The Fool, taken aback, exclaimed, "Why, a little girl who doesn't play games? Nonsense! I won't hear of it!"

Mary Ann shrugged. "Just never saw the point, really."

"But don't you like winning?"

She shrugged again. "Never much saw the point of that, either."

"Clever girl!" the Fool further exclaimed. "However, considering that Hide N Seek doesn't require either a point or a winner, should be a fine fit for a game to play. You do like to play, don't you?"

"Well, of course! Everyone likes to play, don't they? I shouldn't see why I'd be very much different from everyone else in THAT way... but I usually like to play inside where it's safe."

"We can play Hide N Seek inside!"

"Silly Fool! The 'inside' I'm referring to is the inside INSIDE. You know... Behind your eyelids, where nobody else can see. I usually find the most fun playing there."

"That's precisely what I was sporting to," was his only reply.

She responded with a most practical burp.

The Fool took this as a sign to begin playing and generously offered that he would be the first to hide.

She agreed.

"Now close your eyes up tight and no peeking!" he ordered.

Mary Ann covered her face, hands tightly clasped over her eyes.

"I promise not to peek, but..." Her voice trailed off on the wings of a most curious discovery! For even with her eyes closed, she could see every bit of the scene... from the hut and then flying upwards (for it is possible to fly behind one's eyelids) through the chimney, she could see the entrance of That Camp and beyond to the MYSTERY FUNLAND sign and beyond that to places she'd never even been to before! The only thing not seen, she noticed with interest, was herself inside the room of the hut.

"There is no escaping seeing in this dream... ' thought Mary Ann, 'And what a very odd dream it is, indeed! How very much odder that I can't see myself in it.' This caused quite another sort of confusion from the quandaried scene in the looking-glass but a moment ago. She decided finally, 'Ah yes, of course! I'm quite sure that I shan't see myself inside my own dream because my eyes are closed! Silly me!'

This revelation seemed to brighten her spirits quite a bit. Figuring stuff out always made her feel smart. However in all her flying and figuring, she'd forgotten entirely her place in counting.

'Oh dear, now where were we? 47? 69? 91?' Exasperated at figuring stuff out only to lose focus on something as simple as keeping count, she threw her hands in the air figuring it was HER dream after all, so time probably made very little difference anyway.

"Ready or not, here I come!" she shouted, opening her eyes.

The Fool whipped himself around, just a few paces from where he'd started. "Well if you didn't know how to count, you might've just said so..."

"But I CAN count! I can count all the way to a trillion and you know why? Because that's exactly how many stars there are up in the sky tonight... That's why!"

He stared at her, disbelieving.

She continued, only fibbing slightly, "Actually, for your information... There happen to be a trillion and six stars shining, but who's counting..." This last bit of clever wordplay finished with a snicker.

His head drooping in flagrant frustration, the Fool remarked calmly, "As a fool, I have an artistic appreciation for the abstract, of course. But even if you could count to a trillion, which is unlikely for the very fastest of counters to do in a count of 3, how ridiculously impossible a notion it is to conceive that you've counted the stars from inside this hut... with your eyes closed, no less!"

"Nothing is truly impossible, Fool," she defended.

To this he had no reply.

The pixie gal Jag piped in, having been privy to the entire discourse, "How could you have counted ALL the stars in the sky EVERYWHERE by standing in one spot the entire time... And how exactly WOULD you have done that from inside here... With your eyes shut, to boot?"

"Exactly!" the Fool stated, back on his game. "Now, how COULD you do such a thing?"

Mary Ann tried to work through the easiest way to explain that this was all a dream, when it occurred that explaining to people that they're simply figments of one's imagination might come across rudely. She fiddled for a more polite elucidation when the booming voice of the Hatter Fool from inside the looking-glass interrupted.

"LIES! Nothing but lies and madness! Your dreams are nothing but riddles. And a riddle without an answer is madness squared by nothing, my dear!" the Hatter Fool thundered.

The profundity of his accusation cut Mary Ann to the core. She felt a meek tear fall from her closed eye, where behind stars shone ever-brightly still.

She asked unknowingly aloud, "I wonder if God keeps our tears inside a very special bottle somewhere."

"We are God, child," replied the Shaman Ka, walking past.

Mary Ann, realizing now that her words had escaped out loud said most resolutely, "I don't know about that, Shaman. I like to think that God is quite unlike me."

The Shaman Ka stopped with a start. "Whatever for?"

"Because," she continued, "I like to think that God is quite happy."

"Why? Are you not happy, child?" Shaman Ka asked.

"For quite a lot the same reason I don't like to play games or see the point in winning, I guess... Happiness just seems like something that people give quite a lot of harrumphing about. It just never seemed to matter much is all... How happy can I be when there very well are people in other places who are quite UNhappy. All this ME ME ME focus on happiness all the time. Well, it seems arrogant, if you ask me."

"There was another question I'd like to get back to..." pixie gal Jag tried once again. "Enlighten us, please, with this ability of yours to count stars you can't even SEE!" she finished with a laugh.

"I can't decide which riddle is more interesting... The counting of unseen stars or the enormity of a God Bottle that catches fallen tears!" the Fool gushed.

Mary Ann fiddled a strand of hair between her fingers. "It comforts me greatly to think that God collects innocent tears in a very special bottle then pours them back into the world so that new things can grow."

The Shaman Ka bowed before Mary Ann with contended grin.

"That's called 'rain'," corrected Steve, with a nodding Daisy Red Rider in tow.

The pixie gal Jag had clearly had enough riddling for one day. She called out to the room, "Anyone for tea?" and that was the end of that. Everyone vanished for tea time and Mary Ann was left alone, excepting for the Fool who tipped his hat and trailed away, with the wink of an eye that sparkled like a starry night at sea.

CHAPTER SEVEN: THE KOOKOOKACHOO CANOE

During the second round of Hide N Seek, Mary Ann did such an excellent job of hiding that, after the stars outside had cascaded into dawn, she realized with some sadness that the Fool must've have given up looking for her and gone off with the others for tea.

The place she'd chosen to hide was quite clever. She'd climbed up high in the branches of a Deadwood Tree... a good distance away from That Camp. Gazing out across the expanse of land that stretched for miles across, she came to a suddenly unpleasant realization. A rumble from her tummy had made a very persuasive suggestion, indeed.

Her digestion, quite put off from those curiously strong mints and sweet confections, relieved itself in a fitful heave of vomit behind the Deadwood Tree. A bit of regurgitated confection splashed onto her dress, catching her quite off guard. Feeling discomfited now by her slovenly appearance, she wandered off again, away from That Camp. Her only regret was leaving the Fool behind, for he was the first friend she'd ever made that made playing together seem fun, even if he WAS an imaginary friend. She comforted herself in the hope that maybe they might meet again and by then she'd be in a much better state to play.

Hopping along a cleared trail, Mary Ann walked on and on, finally stopping upon a quite unavoidable, very long, curiously bulbous wall. The wall seemed to grow the nearer to it she came, until she was right up close to it, seeing no way round or over it. Most fascinating, it was an impenetrable wall made entirely of balloons.

Removing a pin from her hair, she tried pricking a balloon. Not only did it NOT pop, but instead grew larger, as did the other balloons around it, only increasing the size of the great balloon wall.

Just then, a snide snicker came from behind. She flipped herself 'round quickly to find a most unwelcome sight. It was the Troll... his warty, fat face popping up from a Whilburry Bush.

Nervously she snapped an unpoppable balloon from the wall and began fumbling with its ribbon between her fingers. The balloon pulled her hand up into the air, lighter than a feather. Shocked by this, she released the balloon haphazardly.

"Oh... there you are! Thought you could get rid of me, eh?" snarked the Troll.

"I have no idea what you're talking about... You were the one who disappeared, not me! Though I should say you weren't missed much, if you really must know."

"Oh... I might have guessed. It's not the first time someone has tried to lose a troll, you know." The Troll snickered under his breath. "Seems now you're just as lost as I was! Funny how timing brought us back together... Isn't it, m'lady?"

The thought of being back in the company of the Troll was too dastardly for Mary Ann's already nervous tummy to bear. Without a second thought, she snapped another balloon from the wall and bent down as if to tie her shoe, attaching the balloon ribbon to her shoelaces. The pull of the ribbon lifted her high up... until all she could see was a flying balloon above and beyond that only sky.

Up she flew, away from the ugly Troll. Up the balloon took her high into safe pasture in the clouds. All this floating upside down was quite as dizzying as it was fun, and the tummy flips felt as if they might again repeat those too sweet confections. There was also the issue of wearing a dress and being upside down, which needless to say was quite unladylike (even for an unladylike little girl), so she untied the ribbon from her shoe and clasped it tightly in her hand.

Mesmerized by the sky all about her, she reached out with her free hand to catch a cloud very near. To her surprise, the cloud dissolved as nothing more than wet dewy air between her fingers. She licked the dew to see just what a cloud tasted like (that, and she was also quite parched from fear). Much to her delight, the cloud dew tasted deliciously like fresh bubble gum.

'I like floating in the clouds VERY much, indeed!' thought Mary Ann. 'These clouds are ever-so much friendlier than the ones stuffed up inside my cotton cloud head.' And with that, the clouds weaved themselves together then scooped her up into a soft dewy hammock and rocked her gently to the ground.

On the other side of the big balloon wall, far far away from the Troll, Mary Ann found herself safe once again. Just to be certain of escape, she decided it would be quite smart to keep herself moving in the opposite direction from whence she came. Especially also because though safely away from the unpleasant Troll, she was feeling very lonely and moving always helps pass the time when one is feeling lonely.

The place where she'd landed was a wide open field of grain, with no tree or animal or well, anything for as far as the eye could see, excepting for one thing... one strange particular thing that made absolutely no sense to Mary Ann at all. It was a canoe without any oars, parked just so off to the side of the grain field.

She climbed inside the canoe, trying to configure how a person might maneuver an oarless canoe in a sea of grain... when suddenly, a great sneeze escaped. The sneeze sent her through the grain field... The swhoosh swhoosh of the drifting KooKooKaChoo Canoe making her tummy feel now impossibly queasy. With great drama, she leaned over the side of the KooKooKaChoo Canoe and heaved.

"Oh dear!" exclaimed a voice from behind her.

When she looked up, Mary Ann caught sight of a fat, pouty face attached to a squat chubby body squeezed inside a frilly pink dress. It was a sort of dwarf princess, fitted for royalty with a glittery tiara stuffed tightly betwixt a bush of flaming red hair.

"I say! Well, Helloooooo! I'm the Littlest Princess and this is my pet unicorn Manifesticles!"

She pointed with upturned nose to a stuffed pink toy unicorn, worn from wear presumably from being dragged behind on its sparkly purple leash. Mary Ann felt quite sorry for the poor unicorn, even if it was nothing more than just a toy.

The Littlest Princess continued the introductions, gesturing now with her chubby hand toward two dark figures to her right. "These are my minions... Who cares bother what their names are!"

She curtseyed quite majestically. "Welcome to the Island of Magical Me!"

To this last pronouncement, Mary Ann heaved again.

"Oh goodness, this will not do! Magical minions fetch some nonsense... This girl has turned quite blue!" said the Littlest Princess, obtusely dismayed.

Leaning sickly over the side of the KooKooKaChoo Canoe, Mary Ann glimpsed through a head-ached eye, a smartly dressed ninja standing alongside a black-cloaked fellow. The cloak grabbed at her heel, dragging her face first through the star-sparkled sand and propped her up against a very fat cockatoo.

The Ninja Minion spoke, "However did she find us, Princess? And why's her face so blue?"

The Littlest Princess pinched her nose in disgust. "I say! The dear lass is lagging from that horrid Witch's stench!" Then the Princess waved an imaginary wand over Mary Ann, proclaiming, "You will do as I say! Stop being so blue and come out to play!"

The Princess and her companions waited, drawing closer for inspection, but Mary Ann just moaned, then holding her tummy, rolled over in total collapse, knocking the cockadoodledooo fat on his belly.

"Pa-sha!" cried the Littlest Princess.

"The Witch must have done her a strong spell," spoke the cloak.

"Oh, do shut up, DarkMatter... It's none of your matter! Just fetch me a Rainbow of Hope," snapped the Princess, "Or my anger will splatter!"

"You can control the weather and your minions, my sweet. But perhaps not everything in the entire universe heeds imaginary wands... Especially not REAL magic," the cloaked DarkMatter advised.

The Littlest Princess crumbled her face up into a pursed pout, and with a roll of her eyes and a bat of their glittery lashes, she waved her imaginary wand, transforming DarkMatter instantly into a toad.

Mary Ann looked to the Ninja, who jumped a clear foot in fear, then marched purposely away in no particular direction, presumably to fetch some hope.

As he marched hurriedly along, the Ninja stumbled on his robe. 'How very un-ninja-like!' thought Mary Ann, looking unconvincingly at the Ninja minion.

The Littlest Princess threw her hands up in cupidly cute display exclaiming, "Must I do everything?!" Then off she went, following on the tripped heels of her minion companion, in the wake of an orange-globed sunset.

CHAPTER EIGHT: SWORD OF TRUTH

It was a starry, starry night with skies the color of midnight blue made incandescent by the warm glow of a Tiger Moon. Legend has it that the appearance of a Tiger Moon would bring good fortune to one who had eyes to see it. It was, story told, the very same thing as an ordinary blue moon ... except that it was blanketed with the striped pattern of a tiger. Mary Ann was caught mesmerized inside its poetry, but no sooner did her gaze get caught, then she began to feel a chilly cold breeze from the southeast swathe over her better senses.

Soon Mary Ann started feeling that same familiar pang of loneliness, when she opened her weary eyes to find the very fanciest flower she had ever seen. For not only was it beautiful with the most luminescent color imaginable... delicate pink petals dribbling down into a snow white center with STST pointing out in a very directly phallic way... but then, the tulip petal swayed quite in time with another petal... and that petal with another petal... and so on and so forth.

Within all their swaying, the tulip spoke most swimmingly, "Well, are you just going to stand there staring or will you tell me how perfectly beautiful I am?"

"Oh, but you are MOST beautiful, Miss Tulip! Quite. It's just... I've never seen a tulip speak before and it quite took me off guard, you see."

"How perfectly daft. Little girls can be quite a bore with all their RULES about who can talk and what they think everything should be. It's perfectly obvious that I am a tulip, is it not?"

Mary Ann nodded. "The very most beautiful tulip I think I've ever seen."

"You THINK so, eh? Stupid little girl, what is your name?"

Mary Ann scratched her head, nervously.

"That's funny. I shan't think I rightly remember just now. I've had a belly-full of the sweetest confections just awhile back and they left me quite sick in the head. But everyone here seems to be calling me Alice."

"What THEY call you, eh? Why, don't YOU know your name? My, little girls really are so perfectly daft."

"I do so know my name! It's just that I've forgotten is all... because of those confections, you see..." Mary Ann offered in her defense.

"I SEE. So what we have HERE is actually a simple case of indigestion... Is that it, then?"

44

Mary Ann nodded most emphatically.

"Well now, why in the world would you allow some crazy characters to call you something other than what you ARE?"

"Guess I never really thought too terribly about it... But I wonder." Mary Ann paused momentarily, recounting her adventure thus far. Before she had a moment to think twice about it, out popped an idea, "I do SO know my name! And it isn't Alice at all. My name is Mary Ann!"

"Pleasure to meet you, my dear," Miss Tulip gracefully tipped.

"Pleasure, indeed, beautiful flower!" Then twirling a strand of hair with her fingers thoughtfully, she added, "Do you think these characters are quite mad? I've thought so before but they kept saying it was all in my head."

Miss Tulip yawned. "That sounds very much like what crazy characters do. After all, what is it they say about a pot calling a kettle?"

"Black, I believe."

Miss Tulip cupped the poor child's face with her soft petal, "Yes my girl, that's right. There you are... Right as rain! Why, if anyone's daft AND blind enough to see you as Mad Mary Ann, then they're quite obviously even more daft than the daftest little girl. And daft though they be, little girls do hold the perfect potential to be the most imaginative souls! We call the special ones 'Alice'... Oh, but your name is Mary Ann NOT Alice... That IS correct, is it?"

"Yes, ma'am," she offered honestly. "Alice is the name of my Maemae back home and she is quite a different person with quite an altogether different story, too. My name is Mary Ann, the little daft girl who thinks you're divinely beauuuutiful!"

With this, an unexpected tear plopped down from Miss Tulip's bladed eye onto her soft petal. Out from that tiny drop sprouted a sharp sword.

"Take it, little one... And keep it hidden. It can be perfectly threatening to see a beautiful girl with a sword in her hand. Use it only when you must... To cut through the lies. They are growing like weeds 'round here. Perfectly nasty weeds that kill perfectly beautiful tulips like me from being perfectly beautiful."

"But why?" asked Mary Ann, taking the sword and carefully tucking it inside her coat. "Hey, I know! Why, those weeds are just jealous cowards is all! Hurting beautiful flowers for being more perfect than they are isn't going to make them be any less ugly... Only more so! Has anyone explained this to them?"

"I'm afraid it's perfectly difficult to hear without ears," Miss Tulip explained.

"The weeds are ugly AND have no ears?" Mary Ann said, pulling a face.

"What's the use of having ears when you're made of solid lies? Each weed is its own lie and together they become strong as bamboo and faster to spread, too."

"So then, there's just no use in trying is there, I suppose? We should just let the ugly stupid weeds take over beautiful tulips like you... just like people will keep calling me Mad Mary Ann and Alice and m'lady and things that I quite obviously am NOT. It seems I don't really understand anything anymore. It all seems so strange."

"Everything does as it is, my child. As a flower, I grow perfectly beautiful up up UP. But those perfectly heinous weeds are designed to take over and grow out out OUT. They see beauty in a different way. They, too, are just doing what comes naturally."

"But why doesn't somebody stop them?" Mary Ann pouted.

Miss Tulip pulled her soft petal away with a kiss, "Somebody will."

Mary Ann straightened up her spine and stood at attention.

"I promise not to be so perfectly daft from now on."

"Just remember your REAL name. The more you discover the harder it will be for you to find your way. All you must do is remember your name, little girl. That is the strongest magic in the whole wide world. Remember... No matter what... Who you are."

And with a swoosh of sparkle dust, there appeared the Littlest Princess. She stomped forcefully on the sparkle sand and with her chubby fist to the sky proclaimed, "Who told this Tulip she could speak?" Then to Miss Tulip continued, "And what PERFECT mischief have you been up to?"

Miss Tulip shut up her petals.

"That's right... And stay SHUT!" And with a wave of her imaginary magic wand, the Littlest Princess zipped the lips of Perfect Miss Tulip most perfectly shut.

This made Mary Ann very enraged. She struck the Littlest Princess' imaginary wand with her Sword of Truth, breaking it into stardust. But just as her braveness piqued in pride, cowering fear washed right over in its place.

"YOU.... YOU... B-B-BROKE MY WAAAAA..." wailed the Littlest Princess, stomping her chubby feet, making the ground shake.

The Ninja fell atop DarkMatter who fell right atop the Littlest Princess, creating a stomping clumsy puddle of anger.

Miss Tulip opened her perfectly restored two lips pronouncing, "Run, little girl! Run!"

And without a moment to say their good-byes, she grabbed the sword precariously tipped between a crack in the quaking earth. Grasping it, she fell right through the crack... right inside the belly of the very earth itself.

CHAPTER NINE: RHYMING TIME

So she fell deeper and deeper, until dismayed at long last she thought that perhaps the center of the earth she'd fallen into was a bottomless pit.

In the course of prolonged falling, ticking clocks and whirling thoughts gave space the dimension of such Nothingness that Mary Ann became forgetful of nearly Everything that once had been of any significance. For an instant, she recalled a marvelous dream of a magick floating cat and a curiously kookie house never before seen on her street with a foyer of doors, one slightly ajar, flickering light beckoning from beyond... But just then - A lightning flash of most displeasure knocked her head right side again and the dream slipped away just as fast as it came.

Her wonder turned worrisome as she began again a familiar quandary to test her wits back to the quick.

"Each of these ticking clocks keep ticking time... But it's the same time they tick. Time after time. Constant quarters to ten... How shall I ever know which time is really when? And the whirling spiral I'm caught in is no help... It only tricks me with its contemplelp. I shall rehearse a rhyme to see if it will draw back time or bring me to solid bottom somewhere below... For if I shan't have a Now, I might do very well with a Here."

Quite dizzy from spiraling 'round and 'round, Mary Ann focused on this little rhyme from long ago:

"A boat, upon a stormy see
Lost abyssed most sleepily
In a daydream in July-

Child but one patience to hear.
Eagerly waiting willing ear.
Pleasure mixed in single tear-

Languished sun that born the sky;
Echoes chasing shadows by:
Autumn comforted her cry.

Still they haunt her, monstrouswise,
Always move behind closed eyes
Never seen watchful disguise.

Child, tale yet hid in her tear.
Eagerly waits with willing ear,
Longing for someone to hear.

In Wonderland they said good-bye,
Dreams get lost as days go by,
Dreams get lost as wonders die:

Ever torn between ripped seem-
Lost in tears now torrent stream-
Life, merrily merrily but a dream"

    'Oh dear,' thought Mary Ann, 'I'm sure I got some of that quite wrong. I must try for something easier to recall.' And so, she tried again.

"Humpty Dumpty sat on a hill
Humpty Dumpty had a great spill
All the King's morsels & from the Queen's pen
Couldn't put Humpty right ever again"

    Before she could work out if the rhyme was rightly put, Mary Ann started on a seemingly endless array of questions, which seemed to be more riddling than the rhymes themselves.

    "Why would an egg be sitting on a hill in the first place? That seems quite an unlikely thing for an egg to do! Not to mention the mess an egg makes... However could a person put right a broken egg?"

    Whatever the moral of THAT nursery rhyme was, she couldn't nearly figure. It seemed like a silly notion, all 'round... And that was how every rhyme seemed to turn out.

"Little Jack Horner
Stared into a corner
Dunce cap on his head
Stuck his thumb up his ass
Plucked out a bit of glass
And said "I surely shall be dead!"

*

"Hickory, dickory, dock,
The cat chased down the flock;
The flock got killed,
And blood was spilled;
Hickory, dickory, dock"

    Well, at least that last one seemed to make some sense. Cats do like to chase things that run away then eat them.

Mary Ann stopped momentarily from reciting rhymes and tried remembering her own mind. 'I feel awfully strange... Cold suddenly and quite awfully strange...' And as she looked down into the spiraling abyss once more, searching for some light signaling a bottom or top or any which way out (it was hard to tell which way was up since she'd been tumbling so), she noticed that the sword tucked inside her coat had sliced her delicate arms quite voraciously. In all the rhyming and recalling she must've accidentally cut her porcelain skin to bits!

It was simply too dreadful to bear and just as she pondered the dreadfulness of her current situation, a sharp stinging sang from her wounds. Shaking her to quick awareness, the pain painted a black drop of blood cascading down her arm into the bottomless abyss below. The sight of this caused the poor girl to nearly collapse from shock... Her bloodied little limbs flailing further... tumbling down, down, and down.

PART TWO: THE NIGHTMARE

Lightning rain pours out your eyes
Dread fangs held by the breeze
Turned inside out head lemon squeeze
Dripping ooze on scarred disease
No truth to silence lies

Lies awoken voices dread
Skin pursed prickly, cursing stride
Carried weight, 9 Swords you hide
Then with the 10th, evil abide
To kill the storm instead

Killing loneness crowded cell
Incessant chitter-chatter
Reeks familiar what's the matter
Meanings sought from riddles' Hatter
Ring Rosy round the dell

CHAPTER ONE: EYES WIDE OPEN

When Mary Ann awoke, she found the Mochakie Cat was gone. Gone, as in, died suddenly. Suddenly and strangely indifferent, he appeared to have keeled over on the armrest of the chair she had awoken in, just in front of the fireplace. His sad, lithe body straddling the armrest heavily, eyes shut, never to twirl again. Such was the Mochakie Cat's gifted fate to leave the poor girl now to continue on without his guidance.

An inkling of an idea began to emerge.

'Shall I bury him, then? Is that the smart thing to do?' she thought to herself. Yes. A proper burial sounded right in order. This was to be her first act of solitary magic inside this presently foreboding room inside a home that didn't exist on her street.

Mary Ann drew herself up and out of the chair. Step one. This was quite a feat, considering the fact that gravity seemed to be acting funny. She felt tilted back upon standing, which was most curious. Walking toward the bureau on the far end of the room, her weight shifted slightly and nearly knocked her off-tilt altogether. Panting for breath as she did so, the air was palpable and rich. Step two.

Upon reaching the bureau after much effort in a manner befitting the description of an effortful forward-lean crawl, she was thrown clear back to the other corner of the room. Frazzled from the thrust, Mary Ann felt deep within a vacuumous rising from her throat, which climaxed finally into a thunderous burp.

Remembering her previous situation with the KooKooKaChoo Canoe, she selected another inkling idea... to gulp massive chunks of tender air and stuff it down into her tummy until SWOOSH! - Her body catapulted back to the other side of the room.

Having grasped the first lesson (reversed gravity), she opened the bureau to find a cedar-filled drawer stacked ever-so neatly with fresh, clean white linens. She drew from three stacks... Three equally sized stacks, each one thinner in texture than the next. Step three accomplished.

Taking the linens firmly in hand, she heaved an audible sigh, thinking of the Mochakie Cat and his funny little face, now lifeless, just on the far side of the room. The sadness of her sigh was so great that it enveloped what appeared to be a yawn from inside the fireplace, swallowing her sorrow.

'Oh fiddlesticks!' thought Mary Ann to herself. "There's no conceivable way the fireplace is alive. Now that's just sheer nonsense! I shan't even imagine what in heaven's name is happ--'

But before she could finish her thought, there appeared in the looking-glass above the mantle, a cloud blue sky swimming inside the reflection facing her. As the propulsion of her sigh concurrently pulled her forward, Mary Ann caught a better glimpse into the reflection, drawing her gaze upward towards the ceiling. The ceiling sky as bright as a sunny day in May. The chandelier hanging, poised in the center of the ceiling sky, began to rain plump slow droplets of liquid crystal falling sadly, as is the sky itself were crying.

By this point, she'd reached the armchair where the cat lay. As she knelt over the body, her tears mixed with raindrops falling from the ceiling sky and formed a chorus of dew all 'round.

"I'm ever-so sorry, Mochakie Cat. I didn't know you'd go," Mary Ann whispered softly, placing one of the linens gingerly over him. "And what am I to do now, hmm? What sort of dream is this, anyway... where magic cats die? I don't like it one bit."

And with this, she burst into sobs so deep, they made her small frame shudder with bursts of such intense blue clarity, it signaled at once those lightning storms behind her eyelids again.

A teardrop fell directly onto the thinnest of linens, turning to a swollen red stain as it landed. Confused, she looked up to see that the ceiling sky raindrops from inside the looking-glass were actually crystal shards sharply crashing to the ground. Reaching her hand instinctively to her forehead, Mary Ann grabbed the thickest of linens covering the cat to sop up the blood flowing from her gashed head. No sooner had she lifted the linen, then she found underneath not the cat at all, but a mound of red-eyed, sharp-taloned squirming spiders!

"Oh my goodness, oh my goodness! What IS happ–"

But before she could finish her statement of dismay, a thick greenish black tentacle wrapped itself 'round her tiny ankle and dragged her up and over and upside down.

Facing her reflection, suspended upside down now in the looking-glass, dense smoke drifted over her visage. Then from within a swirl of smoke, appeared a familiar face.

The Mochakie Cat appeared then in the looking-glass, wide-grinned. With a wink of his whirly twirl eye, his friendly smile upturned fiercely... fangs dripping long and sharp down his face, pulling and distorting his grin which said, "Eema realton invisison skowootoon eatoon." And with that, he vanished in a smoke cloud that got sucked up into a pipe that the Fool stood now smoking, propped casually against the fireplace mantle.

"Well, hello again Alice..." he started, cheerfully.

"But my name isn't Alice!" she exclaimed exhaustibly exasperated.

"Why Alice, why? Why must you keep changing? So confusing it is. Glad though I am to see you. And all this fussing about with names and such. Why do you hide behind names Alice, why?"

"I'm not hiding, silly Fool. I'm standing right here."

Then from the distance, a soft voice whispered, "FEAR."

A chill swept through from her head to her toes; the hairs on the back of her neck tickled to attention; the shards on the ground standing upright and peeked. The chills turned to pangs of thorny red fangs, dripping with blood from the tips of the shards soaking the carpet with much too much seeping into her stockings with purposeful stain.

Glancing back up, she noticed that the Fool had moved position very suddenly, indeed. She caught sight of his Hatter Fool self inside the looking-glass. At the far end of the room he stood, grasping the door handle.

"Is that you, Fool?" she asked the reflection.

"Why, of course, Alice sweet Alice, who else would I be but myself?"

'How DID he manage to cross the room so quickly?' Mary Ann thought in her head. 'And my, how he DOES bear a striking resemblance, indeed, to that horrid Hatter!'

"Shall we go on an adventure?" spoke the Hatter Fool reflection with ease, offering his arm in gesture to take. "I say, this place is an absolute bore!"

"I shan't go anywhere with you," she stated tartly to the looking-glass reflection. "Until we have properly met."

"But why Alice, why? A name's just a name. A name is a lie."

"A name's quite important!" she exclaimed directly. "Miss Tulip told me so herself."

"Miss Tulip is far too pretty to be clever," replied the Fool, now again by the fireplace, puffing his pipe.

Mary Ann spun 'round then, bewilderingly excited.

Again now with the pipe, the fireplace stance, Less Hatter than Fool, this looking-glass dance. The confusion between the two sides of Fools didn't ruffle Mary Ann in the slightest, for she was much too taken with curiosity of quite another tack.

'Now how DID he manage to cross the room so quickly, I wonder?' Then she said aloud, "This all seems even stranger and a good bit more terrifying than the dream I just woke from!"

"Merrily, merrily," the Fool he spoke, "Isn't it all but a dream? Alice, my sweet... What do you think, then?" Adding a tip of his fine hat, he continued, "Nothing is what it seems. -Shall we adventure then? Off to tip-toe through the tulips, perhaps?"

"Depart from this place?" Mary Ann said, "Please, Fool, please!"

Off then they went, Mary Ann's arm looped delicately in his. As she did so, she asked patiently this time, "What is your name, Fool?"

"Very well, then." Nothing Fool sighed. "Formularities! Consequentialities and formalities! Semantic and romantics! Precariously pen named... What is your name, child? What is YOUR name?"

'My name...' she thought quite poignantly of the fall, the slashes and dashes to her arm, and her gashed head. 'What a mess I've become! Just a walking hash full of gashes!' And with this last thought, her fingers traced the forehead spot that now felt soft and clean to the touch, perfectly healed.

Curious, indeed!

Still the blood seeped through the carpet below to squishsquish between her stockinged toes. The sight of this made her quiver to the bone, almost forgetting the Fool's question altogether.

Then, back to tack, she announced proudly, "My name is Mary Ann. Mary Ann is my name! And I do hope you appreciate how difficult it's been for me to remember all that... so remember it well yourself."

The Fool said softly, "How could I possibly forget a name as sweet as Mary Ann?"

She blushed, then curiously queried, "What is your name, Fool? Won't you tell me that?"

"Silly child... Really! Don't you know me well enough without a name?"

"Maybe so, Fool. Maybe so. But a name being important, I'd sure like to know."

"Well then... My name is Nothing. Nothing At All!"

"Now why would you go and say a think like that for?" Mary Ann queried further, quite frustrated. Looking 'round the now seemingly serene room, she flailed her arms in dramatic demonstration of frustration adding, "This place is just awful... I do SO wish we'd get out. But first things first... Your name, Fool, confess!"

"Told you once, I'll tell you again. The name is Nothing. Nothing At All."

"Stupid fool!" Mary Ann pouted. "I don't know why I even bother."

"Excellent choice!" he said with a start. "To not bother, that is." After a momentary pause, the Fool cleared his throat adding, "Shall we be off, then?"

And seeing the bloody black shards on the floor all about and the swirling shards that fitted the ceiling in the looking-glass of smoke she thought quite revealing, the poor child thought her options quite dim.

"Fine then, we'll go," she decided finally. "Silly Fool, though... Where will you take me? A place that you know?"

The Nothing Fool laughed. "A place that I know! Child, of course, child! What other place would I take you, but a place that I know?"

"I shan't know anything, I suspect," Mary Ann answered honestly. "I know nothing... Nothing at all."

"Yes! Finally!" remarked the Nothing Fool with glee. "You always were a fast learner, Alice!"

Mary Ann growled.

"Bad joke, pounce!" the Nothing Fool quipped, laughing to himself. Then grasping the door handle, added triumphantly, "A fine adventure, then!"

No sooner had he opened the latch, then a sluthery greenback serpent face popped into view between them slything, "My, but you DO look deliciousssss..."

"Why, I should say!" an exasperated Nothing Fool replied, "Delicious suspicious!"

"Sssssso, you think you're ssssssmart, do you?" glythed the serpent, glaring.

"No, not smart at all," offered Mary Ann tenuously. "He's just a Fool. Pay no attention to him." Then pointing to her chest, added smugly, "I'm in charge here."

The Nothing Fool tipped his sub par hat.

"We just want out of here, really." Growing anxious, she shouted, "Out, out!"

"Isssss that sssssso? Ssssssssmarty pants.... Sssssssay the passssword and you shall passssss."

The hairs on the back of her neck started to twitter; her sopping socks juiced with the oozing black blood from below... She leaned toward the Nothing Fool whispering, "Won't you do something? Do something, Fool!"

"Very well, then. On with the show... Alla ka zoom, alla ka zam! Alacadabra, alla sha ZAM!"

Just then, the doors flew open and the serpent coiled back.

"Ssssssssmarty pantssss...." he said as he slithered back to shadowy pasture.

"Righty-o, then!" the Nothing Fool announced, marching on through.

Mary Ann followed dazily entranced, her feet like lead going clippity clop.

In the Foyer of Doors once more, in the house that didn't exist on her street, Mary Ann noticed that something was off. This hallway was dark and foreboding, save for a single candle, flickering light from above on a swinging candle candelabra. Shadows were strangely traced in front instead of behind, making it ever-so hard to see where one was stepping.

Mary Ann stopped dead in her tracks.

"Well then, here we are!" said the Fool resolutely.

"Here we are?" she asked, dumb-founded. "But we're Nowhere!"

"Exactly! Spot on again, Alice!" cried the Fool with a snarky grin. "So glad you decided to join me on this adventure we're in!"

"For Pete's sake, Fool! Stop with the riddles!" Mary Ann chided. "Just take me someplace safe... Away from this place."

"Oh, away again?" the Nothing Fool asked. Nodding certainly, he added, "Shall we on, then?"

"Well, we haven't gone very far. And besides, this place isn't safe at all. I want to be someplace warm and nice, not here in the dark. I'm terribly afraid of the dark, Fool. Frightens me to the bone."

And no sooner had the words escaped her lips, then the single candle floating above suspended mid-air flickered nearly out.

CHAPTER TWO: THE LOST WALTZ

The Nothing Fool produced a red rose from inside his pocket.

"Alice, Alice, so dramatic. Cobwebs stuffed inside your attic."

She took the red rose saying, "Why Fool, thank you!"

Just then, rose petals from the flower flew majestically up into the air forming a heart floating right before her eyes.

"Oh, it's magical!" she cried.

"Magical, indeed," said Nothing Fool. "Now give me a kiss and I'll show you the safety that you need."

So she pecked him sweetly on the cheek and with the kiss, no sooner had she done so then an "Ouch!" escaped her lips.

For the thorns upon the rose he'd given had grown to prick her soft-formed fingers and seemed to creep up through her arms like vines through her veins up to her heart that beat like a drum.

DA-DUM. DA-DUM. DA-DUMPITY-DUM-DEE-DUM.
DA-DUM. DA-DUM. DA-DUMPITY-DUM-DEE-DUM.

And with the cadence of that drum, the Nothing Fool began marching. He marched right toward a door, just in front of him.

"Well, are you coming or not? I shan't wait all day... Shall we move on from this lot?"

"Oh yes!" she replied, clippity-cloppiting to his side.

He gestured toward the door handle which she obeyingly opened. Through the doorway she stepped into another foyer, the same as before. The door slammed shut behind.

"Oh fiddlesticks!" she touted.

"Oh conundrum," Nothing Fool agreed from the other side. She opened the door once more.

"There you are, Alice, my sweet!"

But her heart had already quickened then to a pace slightly faster.

BA-BA-BUM-CHI-CHI. BA-BA-BUM-CHI-CHI.

To which he marched again.

BA-BA-BUM-CHI-CHI. BA-BA-BUM-CHI-CHI.

More dance-like, he marched straight toward a door to the side. This time she followed, catching his stride. She opened the second door. In stepped the two. No longer trepidatious, they walked right on through. With the door slamming shut as the one had before, they were left in the middle of the next foyer with less light in store.

The candelabra hanging above in mid-air had dimmed to a faint flicker, singing more sadness than aptitude. While the shadows cast before them had grown exponentially and proportionally larger.

"How odd!" Mary Ann said to herself.

"Odd, odder... Foolish fodder," Nothing Fool replied, absurdly mocking.

Her heart raced now, faster now, faster.

DA-DA-DUM. DA-DA-DUM. CHI-CHI-BOOM-BOOM.
DA-DA-DUM. DA-DA-DUM. CHI-CHI-BOOM-BOOM.

By now, the Fool was dancing...

DA-DA-DUM. DA-DA-DUM. CHI-CHI-BOOM-BOOM.
DA-DA-DUM. DA-DA-DUM. CHI-CHI-BOOM-BOOM.

He signaled for her to join the dance. She took his hand and off they went. Danced and pranced in sweet entrance... a waltz so sweet, her heart felt full.

'So beautiful,' she thought, looking in his eyes. Then to the face that held those eyes continued aloud, "I think I can see everything... I can even see myself right through your eyes... I can see myself seeing the very eyes through which I see. I can see us dancing, Fool! How is that possible?"

"Anything is possible," Nothing Fool said in reply, his pool blue eyes turning stone cold. The pupils inside expanding to circumference the whole. Eyes of blackest night he had now... the coldness stretching his face out in escape of wicked laughter.

They danced, though Mary Ann tried to break free. Nothing Fool's now cold-clutched grip would not let her be. As they danced through their shadows, her heart picked up pace.

BA-DID-DEE-DUM. CHEE CHEE. BA-DID-DEE-DUM. CHEE CHEE.
BUM. DEE DUM.

An irregular sort of pattern emerged. Nothing Fool cocked his head to the side, looking displeased.

Stammering for a bit, their dancing of wit ended suddenly as Nothing Fool pulled away and spun off, dancing alone. The poor girl was left quite shaken and chilly by the thrust of his exit spinning with such force as he swept away into his shadow. Her head held heavy and low.

Wrapping her thorny-veined arms all about her in solo embrace, she rocked herself as she held on for dear life, sinking into a pathetic puddle on the floor. She rocked herself straight into a tizzy. Left alone now in the dark, her mind felt quite dizzy.

"I do not like it here... I do not like it here," was all she could muster. Then inwardly to herself, 'There must be a door that leads out from here. Even the door back to that terrible serpent would be of more comfort than this darkness. Any door would do. I just needs must find light... Away from this cruel candle which doesn't burn bright.'

Her heart now beat with a rhythm so faint, it murmured.

BA-DA-DEE-DUM. CHEE-CHEE BUM. CHEE.
BA-DA-DEE-DUM. CHEE-BUM. CHEE-BUM. CHEE-BUM.

The beat of her heart seemed as lost as she, searching for the Fool's lost waltz. So on her hands and knees she crawled, reaching through the shadow before her... feeling nothing but darkness on all sides. She reached out for something... anything... beyond the darkness, for what seemed like an eternity.

CHAPTER THREE: WISHES AND A SWIMMING CIRCUS

Crawling in the darkness for what seemed like an eternity (it was really only about fifteen minutes), Mary Ann felt so cold and so afraid that all she could think about was how cold and how afraid she really was. Finally her thoughts turned somewhat more willful. Just as soon as the next thought popped into her sad little head, she spoke it out loud, for fear of losing it.

"All this going alone in the worst possible kind of fashion. Where are all my little friends like Wolf and Owl NOW? Someplace warm and safe and fun, no doubt. I wish I was someplace warm and safe... having fun."

And just like that, a laugh burst forth from her like a thunder clap through her cloudy sad head. From that quite wicked-sounding laugh came a tingling sort of sensation and from somewhere deep inside, a still small voice whispered, "STAND UP." Without knowing why precisely, she obeyed.

Within a nanosecond of stumbling to her feet, Mary Ann found that she felt a good bit better. The ground was decidedly damp she realized now and being upright suited her balance more definitely.

"Thank heavens!" she announced to no one in particular. "Now if only I could see where in blazes that I'm walking, maybe I'd get somewhere... or at least see where it is that I've been... or find some sort of direction! I do SO wish there was some small bit of light to show me where I am."

No sooner had the words escaped her lips, than the teensiest "EEP!" peeped from beneath her feet. Lifting them one at a time, she checked under each foot carefully. And there, squished on her right sole, she found a firefly gasping for air.

"Eep! Eep!" went the firefly with a big, fat frown on his face.

"Oh NO! What have I done?" she chastised herself, gently stroking the ailing firefly's broken wing. "How dreadfully awful. How totally and completely... How... How... How am I seeing you, little firefly?"

The firefly simply replied, "EEP!"

Still not quite grasping the point, the pure-hearted little girl with the stuffy little head said, "Oh eepy firefly, I'm ever-so sorry to have stepped on you. I couldn't see you, you see. It's been ever-so dark and I'm quite lost and it never occurred to me that someone might be there under my feet."

"EEP!"

"Oh, you poor, poor firefly! I do wish you'd feel better so you could fly again!"

And no sooner had the words escaped her lips, than the eeping firefly swung into the air and swooshed around her thrice. In doing so, she laughed a far less wicked sort of laugh and sighed with calm relief that she now had, after long last, found another friend.

Onward they went from there, Mary Ann taking careful steps as they did so, for she could only see just a hair beyond where her next step would be... by the slightest light of the firefly.

She was fairly exhausted now from so much travel and half-spun by where the Nothing Fool had gone and why on earth she had been left there alone, stumbling about in the dark.

Mary Ann said to the firefly, "None of this makes a lick of sense at all. Not one thing, I tell you! Can you tell me, please... Might you explain to me what's happening here? You do look ever-so smart. I think I shall call you 'Professor'... that's just how smart you seem."

Professor Firefly answered, "EEP!"

Frustrated, she continued, "Oh, jibber-jabberish! Quit with that jammering on of the eep eeping... It's quite a bit silly in a maddening sort of way. Can't you speak English?"

"EEP!"

"Never mind, then," she said emphatically. "No more from you. I was hoping that you could be my traveling chum, but all that EEPing is nothing more or less than grating on my nerves."

A brisk breeze wafted from the easterly direction, sending a chill up her spine.

"Oh fiddlesticks! Cold again! I must say, it's been such an awfully strange day. All I want is to know what's happening... Is that too much to ask?" She looked hard at the Professor, "Well, is it?"

"Eep."

"Yes yes... You eep as if I could understand a lick of what jibberish it is that you're saying. If you could speak ENGLISH or even French... for I studied a bit of that in school back home. Otherwise, don't speak. Eeping just confuses me all the more. And I'm quite confused enough, if you should care to know."

"Eep eep," said Professor Firefly consolingly in return. He spun through the air and landed on her index finger, holding it with his once broken wing.

"Oh Professor, thank you. I know you're not trying to annoy me. It's just that being friends with someone who doesn't speak the same language as you is quite bothersome, you see. If you were human like me then we could walk and talk, like people do... but since we can't understand one another, it all just seems rather pointless."

The Professor nodded.

Mary Ann pet his tiny soft back.

"Wouldn't it be ever-so much better if we could find a light switch to this place? And if you could speak English or French, then maybe you could tell me where that might be. You see... clear communication is quite important with these things. But I suppose I can want all that I want but that won't make my wishes come true. Mother was right. She used to say, 'Child, when will you learn? Wishes are for fishes.' Or was it... 'Wishes for fishes?' I never can quite recall Mother's sayings exactly. Though they usually are spot on correct."

But before the Professor could mutter an eep, Mary Ann followed his gaze 'round behind them where a largely ballooned clown fish swam right before her very eyes.

"Oh, good heavens! Things just get stranger and stranger..." Just then, her sentence of awed amazement was interrupted by a teeming school of fish holding what seemed to be a floating circus.

"Well now, that certainly is something!" she exclaimed, quite excited that now at least they had traveling music.

"Do you hear that, Professor? Now we can dance instead of walking!"

And with that, the firefly smiled.

"It is, isn't it? Ever-so much more nice to dance?"

The Professor bopped to the rhythm of the great trumpet being played by a fat blue blowfish.

"Don't you wish we had more light, though... so that we could dance more freely? Wouldn't make much of a difference to you, I realize... being that you're flying and all. But walking and dancing is much more complicated a task than flying and dancing is."

Professor Firefly swooped to the ground and (being that he was her only source of light) she stopped alongside him. He began strutting beside her, dance-walking in her forward shadow.

"Oh, I see. How clever. Fine, then. Dance-walking you can do quite smartly, Professor... Nicely done. But this showing off of yours is certainly not making it easier for ME to walk or dance at all, with your little light being all the way down THERE. It was much easier when you were beside me."

So up flew the firefly once more, just a hair ahead of her, fly-dancing to light the way.

"How it is that you understand me, Professor, and yet I don't get a lick of your EEPing? It's so utterly infuriating!" And with that, she heaved a deep sigh of frustration. With that sigh came a swoosh of cold breeze that waft the firefly out of view entirely.

"I'm sorry, Professor! I didn't mean to get angry! I don't know why I say the things that I say sometimes... I simply don't know whatever is wrong with me! Nothing makes sense at all and I'm just so frightened and confused. Please come back... Please!"

She felt tears reaching up from her heart through her a frog in her throat. The sound of thunder threatened from beyond.

"No, no, NO! No more thunder and no more tears! I'm tired of those thunderclaps that burst in my ears! Professor and Fool, where have you gone to? Why have you left me so lonely and blue?"

Mary Ann parked herself in a heap. Little sense in continuing, she realized, with no light any longer to guide the way. The way to where she had no idea. She could, of course, resume crawling but she very much disliked that option. Crawling hurt her knobby knees.

"Please come back, little friend! Oh, please don't be cross with me... Why, o why must everyone LEAVE me all the time? Especially when I need them most? I do SO wish you'd come back and that there was sun to see where we might be. That is, if fireflies can dance in the daytime... I'm not quite sure."

And just like that, Professor Firefly came back and with him, the brightest globe of a sun Mary Ann ever had seen.

66

CHAPTER FOUR: THE MYSTIKAL MISFITS

Onward they went, with the fish clown circus... marching and dancing, and in all of their marching and dancing, Mary Ann had inadvertently dropped her Sword of Truth from inside her jacket. She hadn't in truth even noticed it was gone, so caught up she was in all her wishing. For now that she'd caught on to just how powerful her wishing was (and smugly contended to prove her mother wrong) Mary Ann was having a daisy of a time creating all SORTS of new things!

She wished, for instance, for this shade which she sat underneath. 'Twas a tall tree that offered this shady respite from a quite light, and quite hot sun overhead. In taking this short rest, Mary Ann realized she could do with something to quench her parched thirst.

"I wish I had something cold to drink in," she announced, expectantly.

And with that, the fish clown circus led her straight to a camp, which now appeared just thirteen paces ahead.

It looked to Mary Ann to be nothing more than a bar saloon, really, with a sign post out front, just ahead of the stairs, that read "MYSTIKAL MISFITS." Next to the sign post stood a pulley, attached to what she couldn't see. But seeing no other way, she tugged the pulley and as she did so, a red carpet swirled out before them.

Peeking her head inside the room, she queried curiously, "Hello? Hello? Is there anyone who might have some lemonade for me?"

Out from the corner of her eye, the tree had come to life and moseying on up to her said, "You want some lemonade, huh? Well, whaddya gonna give me then in exchange for it?"

"Give you? Why, I shan't know..." she stammered in reply, then to the Firefly, "What's a lemonade going for these days?"

"Don't bother asking him," said the Tree Man in a snarky tone. "He doesn't know anything. Why just look how small his stupid little brain is."

The Firefly didn't like that bit of conversation one bit, so he flew straight up to the Tree Man's nose and stuck a stinger right there, red as a rose. Outraged, the Tree Man swatted Professor Firefly and he fell, lifeless to the ground.

Mary Ann composed herself, and thus declared, "I wish that Professor Firefly were alive again and someplace safe away from you," she said, pointing to the tree. "And furthermore I'd like that you would please be ever-so good as to give me some lemonade. For what in exchange, I surely don't know... whatever a Tree Man needs, I can't scarcely imagine!"

And with that, Professor Firefly disappeared, seemingly to safer pasture. The idea that the Firefly was gone bothered Mary Ann, but not ever-so much more than seeing him get hurt, so she felt decidedly confident about her decision to wish him away. Still, this Tree Man puzzled her. She hadn't, after all, wished for a snarky Tree Man but instead for a lemonade to drink... isn't that right?

"Now listen here, mean Tree Man..." she began.

"Yes, yes... your lemonade. Blah, blah, blah. What makes you think we got lemonade here?"

Mary Ann replied, quite a bit enraged now. "I made a WISH for it, you stupid oaf! Now, it should be around here someplace..." she continued, off presumably in search of something resembling lemonade from behind the saloon bar counter.

"Hey, hey, hey..." spoke up the barkeep, appearing quite unexpectedly from behind the other side of the counter. Then to the Tree Man, "What's all this about then, eh?"

Mary Ann fluffed her stained, spoiled dress and stepped forward. "This is ABOUT a wish for some lemonade is all. I asked the Tree Man for some, but all he does is swat poor, innocent fireflies and ask stupid questions. I wished for a cold lemonade to drink, is the thing." Then remembering her manners added, "My name is Mary Ann, by the way. How'd you do?"

"Well hello there Mary Ann! Fine of you to drop in. But look see here, little girl... This ain't no self-serve bar we be runnin' here, mate. And that TREE MAN you're talkin' about there happens to be our Ringmaster."

"Ringmaster? I dare say... Ringmaster of WHAT?!"

But before the barkeep could answer, the flying fish circus came bumbling in, trumpeter in tow. They swam straight up to the bar and plopped themselves (the entire flying circus!) right into a giant cherry bowl.

"Well now, where'd these fellas come from, then?" asked the barkeep.

Mary Ann answered proudly, "I brought them. They're with me."

"With you, then, is it? How's that, mate?" questioned the barkeep.

Mary Ann stomped her feet in frustration. "I keep trying to TELL you that... I simply wished them into existence and there they were. As I wished for that glass of lemonade I'm still quite waiting for."

By now, the Ringmaster had climbed out of his tree costume, for that's all that it was... nothing more than a silly costume with stilts. As he stepped down off the stilts, Mary Ann found out that the Ringmaster was a good foot shorter than she. She was thinking of how funny a thing that was when...

"Soooo, you can make wishes, eh?" the Ringmaster queried with a smirk.

"Well, I say! I'm no liar, sir," Mary Ann retorted.

"How'd your dress get so mussed up then, mate?" the barkeep questioned, surveying her suspiciously.

"Never mind that," she answered, folding the stained bit of her dress into her left hand. 'Now, about that lemonade..."

"Yes, how about that lemonade," the Ringmaster stated, saddling up next to her at the bar. "Funny that you can wish things into existence, but that here you are... in a bar that serves absolutely no beverages whatsoever."

"But why ever would you keep a bar in the middle of the desert if you're not going to serve beverages? I do say... that's not very clever."

The barkeep became rustled over her last bit of statement, but before he could retort, the Ringmaster stopped him with a cool hand in the air that signaled stop.

"Perhaps so. But then, maybe you should try again... with your clever wishing skills for that fresh, cold lemonade. Why, would you mind ordering me one, too? It DOES get SO dry out here in the desert without anything to drink." His eyes glanced her over up and down.

Mary Ann, nervously bunching the entire front part of her spoiled dress in a ball with both hands now, added, "I think I shall try again, thank you very much. But as for you, I do not know. What will you give ME in exchange for a lemonade, sir?" (She thought this last bit ever-so clever.)

"Oh, well that's simple," the Ringmaster said with a curtsy. "I'll give you a tour."

For whatever reason she didn't know, the barkeep seemed now quite put out by the Ringmaster's offer for a tour. Whatever the reason, she thought herself very special to be given one... tours being ever-so exotic a sort of thing.

"Deal," she agreed resolutely.

"Excellent!" the Ringmaster smirked in return.

Then clearing her throat, she pronounced in a rather lackadaisical way, "I wish for two lemonades. One for me and one for my friend the Ringmaster."

Just as she said it, two glasses of ice cold lemonade appeared before her, suspended for but a moment in the air before falling to the ground and spilling all over what was left of the clean spots on her pretty little doll dress.

"Oh dear!" gasped the Ringmaster. "Gonna hafta be more clever than that!"

"Very well, then," Mary Ann said crossly. Now focusing closely on her word choice, she continued, "I wish for two cold lemonades to sit upon this bar stand here in front of me."

Two elephant-shaped tumblers appeared before her with ice cold lemonade teeming from inside the cups.

She picked up the elephant tumblers, and handing one to the Ringmaster, took the other, and sipped delicately from the elephant-trunk straw. But the lemonade wouldn't seep up the straw... so she sucked a good bit harder this time, pursing her cheeks so, but still, nothing.

"Try using your tongue," the Ringmaster offered. "Like this..." and he demonstrated a most disgusting-looking trick with his tumbler.

Mary Ann shuddered. "No, but thank you. I'll drink my lemonade my own way, thank you very much." And with that, she sipped from the side of the elephant's bottom at the OTHER end of the tumbler.

Finishing it off in two big gulps, Mary Ann slammed her empty elephant tumbler on the bar counter.

"Now then, about that TOUR," she declared, suddenly feeling quite fuzzy in the head.

The Ringmaster grinned, bowing though not lowering his head from her gaze.

"I thought you would never ask..." Then, he turned to her with a shrug of the eyebrows and smirk that quite reminded Mary Ann of the Nothing Fool.

Remembering him again suddenly, she asked, "Do you suppose you know which way the Nothing Fool might have gone? That is, if you know of the Nothing Fool... Do you then, Ringmaster, sir? I lost him awhile back and it would be ever-so lovely to see him again."

The Ringmaster chuckled inwardly, "Nothing Fool? Yeah, I know him... What's it worth to you to know where he is?"

Mary Ann's face grew red. "YOU and your INCESSANT bargaining! I was simply asking a very decent sort of question. You needn't make EVERYTHING into a deal exchange. It really comes off quite rude."

The Ringmaster shrugged. "I don't know why you'd want to bargain for a fool like that, anyway. All he talks is nonsense. Quite full of himself, if you ask me."

Mary Ann pouted then under her breath, "You should talk."

"What?"

"Oh nothing," she remarked. "Nothing at all."

The Ringmaster snarled. "INDEED." Then pointing to the curtain to his left, added, "Shall we?"

Mary Ann nodded. "Just one moment please..." then closing her eyes, she imagined aloud, "I wish for a pretty new dress," (her mind wandered) "with ribbons all about it and a short trim of pretty lace and..." (now her imagination really got reeling) "new pretty black patent leather shoes with a thrice heel..." (she'd always wanted to be taller and then would be even bigger than the nasty Ringmaster if she grew in stature) "... and I would like red hair instead of this mousy brown color..." (always having wanted to know what being a redhead felt like) '... so I wish for a head full of luscious red locks, and... and..."

"AND?!" the Ringmaster spat onto the ground.

"I DO WISH YOU WOULD SHUT UP!" And before she knew anything at all, the Ringmaster's face turned shutter-like into tiny little windows that twisted closed upon themselves into a sort of black hole. So shocked by this, she scarcely noticed that she herself had changed quite convincingly to look not one iota much like herself at all. Nor, it deserves mentioning, did she remember the very last part of her intended wish in the first place (before she got her mind to wandering about new dresses with ribbons and fancy shoes to make her taller), which was, of course, the wish of Mary Ann's heart, which was, of course, to see the Nothing Fool again.

She lifted the curtain, which the Ringmaster had been ever-so kind to point out before he was shut up entirely, and walking behind was immediately greeted by a face so fat that it was hard to focus on more than one eye at a time.

It was no matter for the eyes themselves were quite crooked and totally disproportionate in size. Then again, come to think of it, everything about this 'it' was disproportionate. The right leg stood a good head longer than the left, to which was attached a most fantastic marble-carved club foot, fashioned into the likeness of a hammer. The left arm hung, hand clipped to its belt, quite like a pocket watch and the right arm nothing more than a short stub poking out grotesquely from a hairy, stinky armpit. On its shirt was written the word "404", which Mary Ann assumed to be its name.

Being that as it may, she had learned from her mother that assuming things only makes one an ass for some reason or other (she couldn't recall the details), and so she thought to ask, "Well, hello there. My name is Mary Ann... How'd do you? I'm just traveling through here, you see. What is your name, sir, if you please?"

"Bob. It is ma'am, sir, not sir, ma'am it is. Now you know here know you now."

"Oh, I see," Mary Ann replied, though she silently wished she didn't for how horrid-looking this poor creature was. What she didn't realize was how twisted her face had become in expression, in thinking such a thought.

"Take a picture it will last longer last will it picture a take," Bob with the 404 grumbled. "Hiding behind that costume that behind hiding. Think maybe you are so smart so are you maybe think!"

"Seems quite the opposite, actually... The more I think, the less I seem to know. And the more I know, the less smart I think I am. But I notice you're wearing a number on your shirt. What's the figure signify?" Mary Ann queried.

"Why, 404 is what I do I what is 404, why!"

"I shall call you Bob with the 404, then!" Mary Ann declared. "If you don't mind, that is... Putting what you do into your name is a very clever introduction, indeed!"

"As if you have not already done so on the page the on so done already not have you if as..." Bob with the 404 touted, "... Storytellers need never ask, only listen only, ask never need Storytellers."

"Thank you, Bob with the 404! I shall remember that from now on, smart friend."

Walking just between them, a human-sized chicken clucked by, then again back... and back again, clucking all the way back and forth like that, pacing.

Mary Ann snuck her head around the clucking chicken to Bob with the 404 and said apologetically, "Ever-so my mistake, I do apologize... Sincerely so."

Bob nodded. "I should think so if so think should I. It is obvious enough that enough obvious is it. You might watch what is happening is what watch might you. That is that. It ever gives me pain me gives ever it."

She tossed a lock of curly red hair from her face, and confused she confessed, "Whatever that should mean, I'm not certain for I do have the tendency occasionally to be daft. But I am sorry for causing you pain. Now, I have said sorry and so, there you are! I meant no harm whatsoever." Then to the clucking chicken, "Now then, I do say, what are YOU going on about? Clucking about creating a disturbance, getting everyone all riled up?"

The chicken stopped dead in his tracks. "It's just that I'm in a quandary, it seems. I had a striking notion to cross over to the other side of the street, you see... but then the fire guzzler asked me what for... and well, I can't seem for the life of me to remember! Do you suppose if you were a chicken, why it is you might want to cross the road?"

Mary Ann tossed her head in triumphant display. "I shan't know WHY exactly, but seeing as there is no road, I don't much see what difference it should make at all."

"No road?" The chicken looked puzzled. "How very odd!" he added, doing a double take. Then checking his pockets, added again, "It was here just a moment ago..."

Bob with the 404 shook his fat, ugly head saying, "No use trying to dig to trying use no. I have some have I. Prankster Pricken that one is nothing more nothing is one that Pricken Prankster."

"Why, I do say, whatever that means... Well, I should say that I agree."

Bob snorted, "You are welcome are you."

The clucking Prankster Pricken Chicken popped up then in her face, "Would you know then, the answer to my riddle? I have another... for you see I am forever mixing things up, it seems. Mightn't you clear up another matter for me, then?"

"I shall try but I can't promise much these days, I'm afraid," Mary Ann confessed.

"Just whatever you can do would be a might jolly appreciated. It's this business with the Egg... Forever fighting we are over who got here first. He absolutely INSISTS that he got here first... And I wouldn't bother much with it at all, but there is the matter of who should get top bunk in the barracks and whosoever got here first should be tossed to the bottom."

"Well if you should want to be on top then I would say you might have wanted to come after then," Mary Ann replied logically, which sent the chicken reeling with laughter. Mary Ann, not having the foggiest notion of what was so funny, added smartly, "But I might consider your riddle, if you can answer mine. I've been working on it for some time now to no avail on my own. So you see, here it is: Why is a raven like a writing desk?"

Having said it out loud, Mary Ann suddenly remembered the Nothing Fool disguised as a hatter and before the Prankster Pricken Chicken could get a solid answer to her riddle, she announced loudly, "I WISH FOR NOTHING FOOL TO JOIN US HERE RIGHT THIS VERY INSTANT!"

And no sooner had she wished it, there he was swinging in a hammock just to the left of Bob with the 404 to the rear.

"Fool! Oh, Fool! How very glad I am to see a friendly face!" Mary Ann leapt over to him, jumping on the hammock, causing it to crash to the ground.

Nothing Fool stood, brushing himself off, "I do say, Alice... I do say!"

"I'm just beside myself with joy, Fool... That's all! I'd wondered where you'd gone from before and then all this wishing business started and... Oh, Fool! You will SO love the wishing business! It's ever-so useful, though I've learned to be quite particular about the things I wish for and to pay close attention not to forget my name and be mistaken and things."

"Ah yes," Nothing Fool agreed, "Stuff N Things. Stuff N Things!" Propping his hat upright on his head, then tilting it just so to the side, he continued, sizing her up. "Why, whatever has HAPPENED to you, Alice? I say, you look dreadfully horrid. Red hair most certainly does not become you, m'dear." Then, seeing the others for the first time, thrust forward his hand. "How d'you do? How d'you do?", shaking first the chicken's wing and then Bob with the 404's arm nub.

"How d'you do?" they replied in chorus.

From above, swinging down on a trapeze in most elegantly graceful display, waft a dazzling brilliant gem of a gorgeous creature effortlessly easing in.

"How d'you do?" she oozed.

Immediately, Nothing Fool's gaze turned to the gorgeous creature of dazzling brilliance. Catching his stare, she straddled up next to his side, wrapping her svelte stature up against his torso.

"Good now, thanks," she quartered breathfully. Nothing Fool stood ripe at attention, eyes wide, smiling toothlessly.

"Say," began the Prankster Pricken Chicken, "We were just debating which came first. The chicken..." he said, pointing to himself, "or the Egg. When you two..." he said, pointing to the Fool with the bedrilling trapeze artist draped to his side. The Prankster Pricken Chicken nodded knowingly at the Fool, "You wouldn't happen to know anything about riddles, would you?"

The Nothing Fool blushed, his face masking the sincerity of his steady heart. "I know a thing or two... I do!"

Bob with the 404 piped in, "Is that so that is? A Fool knows nothing knows a Fool... This is why Fools are loved so loved are Fools why is this."

The Prankster Pricken Chicken continued, "Well, you might be able to help me out, then. Which is it, Fool? Which came first the chicken or the egg?"

Nothing Fool perked to (somewhat distracted by the enchantress on his... well, entwined on his... well, that is to say, distracted) and straightening his half-cocked tie replied, "I should say, that's a pretty good one, indeed! Now I might consider giving yours a good go - because it IS rather clever - If you might answer me this teensy query first... It's been riddling me so!"

The Prankster Pricken Chicken stiffened. "All right. Give it a go..."

Nothing Fool smirked, his eyes turning grim, "Do you happen to know... Why might a raven be like a writing desk?"

"Oh, how funny!" the Prankster Pricken Chicken said, surprised. "That's just EXACTLY what SHE riddled!" clucking in Mary Ann's direction.

Nothing Fool's face grew discernibly stern. "You've stolen my riddle, have you? Why, Alice, that simply won't DO! Everyone to their own riddles, I dare say... Really! I suppose next you'll be stealing my hat, then, will you?" he finished, settling his sub par hat steadily on his head.

The brilliant dazzling creature tsk!tsk!ed in accord, her thin fingers gracefully tracing sideway eights on Nothing Fool's chest.

Mary Ann growled under her breath, for she really didn't like the way Nothing Fool was suddenly acting around this seductive acrobat.

The Prankster Pricken Chicken clucked in just then, "Oh, I have it! Ravens and writing desks... Yes!" he clucked in approval. "Clever, that one."

"THANK YOU," Nothing Fool pronounced loudly in Mary Ann's direction.

"Yes... Very clever indeed," the Prankster Pricken Chicken continued. "For, you see, a raven and a writing desk are like one another in not one, but two ways. Oh yes, you see... for the raven like the writing desk are both THINGS, firstly. And then secondly, you see... both the raven and the writing desk also both make a "rrr" sound when you say them, which is quite nice. You should try it."

So Bob with the 404 and the Prankster Pricken Chicken joined in chorus, murmuring "Rrr... rrr... rrr..."

"Excellent try, I must say," Nothing Fool interrupted, "But incorrect, I'm afraid." And with that, he sat. The bredazztarly critchure plopped directly into his lap, wrapping her arms 'round his neck.

"But I like the way you think, chicken man." Then to the Fool, the brilltestingly bilcher abacodat added smoothly, "And I love the way you..." at which point, the bridizzlying cripture whispered something (apparently quite funny) into his ear.

Nothing Fool's half-cocked laugh sent shivers up Mary Ann's spine. It was rather grotesquely obscene, the way the Fool allowed himself to be fondled by this bedastardly acribet.

Daring to catch his attention on more IMPORTANT matters, she interrupted their drippingly sickening chatter.

"So then, about that wishing, Fool... Would you like to see how it works? It really is QUITE impressive!"

But the Nothing Fool made no acknowledgement of her whatsoever, so caught up was he in the smooth stroking of his... well, that is to say... The Fool's attention was quite engaged in other matters.

"Excuse me, ma'am?" she tried again, interrupting.

The brilling arcibad turned smoothly toward Mary Ann. "None necessary whatsoever, my darling."

To this, the Nothing Fool giggled. Mary Ann thought the whole business quite rude. The 'darling' mention snapped back to mind the Lala woman from the Land of Lost Toys, reminding her again of the nursemaid back home, conjuring most unpleasant remembrance of those dreaded marching towers that doused her medicinally. She cleared her throat, regaining some composure.

"Mother always says that not introducing oneself when joining a social gathering is a display of bad upbringing. And well, since I wouldn't DREAM of behaving in such a manner, I'd very much like to introduce myself," Mary Ann began.

Nothing Fool chimed in, "Always with the names, she is... Consequentialities, I say... What a BORE! Meanwhile, she steals my riddle then wants to make up for it by showing me a parlor trick! Fishy wishing, indeed!"

Mary Ann piped in then, "But the wishing really WORKS! No simple parlor trick, either... I can assure you that! And I didn't steal your riddle, I didn't... I was simply trying to solve it for you, Fool!"

"Leave it to an Alice to explain wishes, tricks, and riddles!" Nothing Fool exclaimed to the small, misfit congregation, leaving them all stitched up in laughter.

Having grown now quite past exasperated, she stomped off, but not before yelling right to his face, "MY NAME IS NOT ALICE, YOU STUPID FOOL!"

Trailing behind, Nothing Fool's voice called back, "IT IS SO! YOU'RE JUST NOT SEEING THINGS RIGHT, ALICE! ALL THAT WISHING HAS GONE TO YOUR HEAD... WAKE UP, ALICE! OPEN YOUR EYES!"

Without even a glance back towards him, she retorted, "It's my wishing that brought you here, Fool... Just remember that! And my eyes are quite open inside this dream, thank you very much!" With that, she stumbled over a lone, large rock sitting directly in her path.

She shook off the square audacity of the rock, and stepped with highbrow gait 'round it, then marched off, tears welling up and streaming down, falling tearful well-springs of sorrow upon her blue ribboned dress.

CHAPTER FIVE: THE GNOME AND HIS WIFE

Mary Ann wandered off alone again, not knowing which way to go or what to do or what to wish for... not knowing very much anything at all. In fact, the only thing for certain she could definitively pinpoint was this stinging pain in her heart that felt ever-so much like the Fool's thorny rose prick. That, and the quite obtuse vines twisting up her bulging veins, causing her to tug at her sleeves to cover their putridity.

"I am, just as 404 said, ever-so ugly, aren't I? And whatever 'insipid' means I shan't know, but that as well, surely," she spoke aloud to herself (for she was the only one presently to speak to). Clasping her vine-veined arms 'round her, tucking in tightly from a bitter cold breeze familiar as before, there from the blustery distance, a rumbling thunder tumbled.

"No, no, NO!" cried Mary Ann to no one but herself. "No more thunderstorms inside my head or anywhere! No more lightning, no more teeth! No, no, NO!" And with this final no-ing, she wished for the only conceivable thing that might make the situation better - which was, of course - a warm, safe fireplace with a spot of amber tea.

Having wished for these things already, Mary Ann added, "And nice, kind people THIS TIME, if you please!"

And just like that, appeared a log cabin perched on the end of a lane. How she knew it was a corner house is most curious, indeed, seeing as there were no other dwellings about, but it was none-the-less a corner lot cabin. In front of the cabin hobbled a half-bent gnome clutching a cane. Presently, he looked up and seeing Mary Ann all covered in gloom, quickly baited to her aid.

"Oh. Oh dear! Dear me... Looky what we have here!" the Gnome started awkwardly.

By now Mary Ann was growing quite weary of the formal consequentialities of introducing one's self over and over again, and being quite chilled to the bone beside, she said simply, "Mary Ann's the name, sir. How'd you do? I hate to be so abrupt, but would you mind ever-so much pointing the way to the fireplace and the tea?"

The Gnome shook his head in bemusement.

"Why yes... Of course. Of course! Tut! Tut!" as he ambled to her side, barely able to walk himself. He was, upon seeing this gesture, a very kind man, indeed, she decided. The Gnome ushered her in and sat her down in a rocking chair beside the fireplace, tossing a soft wool blanket to cover herself up in.

"Tea, woman!" he decreed kindly. And out from behind him popped the sweetest looking lady whom Mary Ann thought must assuredly be the Gnome's Wife.

"I'm coming, I'm coming..." the Gnome's Wife tuttled, stopping short beside her. "Why, what do we have HERE?"

The Gnome answered, "I know... Said the same thing myself. I just found the poor thing outside, shivering to the bone. She's looking for a fireplace and some tea. Can we keep her, dear?"

Before the Gnome's Wife had a chance to reply, Mary Ann cut in, "I'm not sure about KEEPING me, but I would so like a chance to catch my breath, if you please," she said (mostly to the wife, for everyone knows to check with wives on such things). "Just a short rest and I'll be on my way," she promised, criss-crossing her heart.

"Her name's Mary Ann," the Gnome tuttled. "Such a NICE name, isn't it?" Then nodded to himself, in agreement.

The Gnome's Wife seemed then to go about her own business as before, quite as if Mary Ann wasn't even there. Mary Ann thought for a moment that is WAS a bit rude, wasn't it? Dropping in on these gnome people, ordering tea? What MUST they think? But kind people, gnomes or not, tend to overlook such things and so it was. Quite comfortable.

"We only have the one tea, dear," the Gnome's Wife said matter-of-factly. "But then, I suppose you'll be fine with amber tea?"

Mary Ann's face softened into a nod as she rested her tear-wearied face gently into the soft wool blanket. The Gnome scuttled about, this way and that, finally producing a foot stool with great glee, which he tenderly propped under her feet.

"You are ever-so kind, sir. Thank you."

The Gnome blushed. "Tut. Tut. Are you settled, then?"

"Oh, yes. Quite," said Mary Ann, yawning.

"Good," was his reply, so sweet that it dried up what was left of her sorrow.

"Whatever are you doing, old goat? Come help me in the kitchen!" spake his wife.

The Gnome stood up, brushing dust from his trousers and proceeded accordingly to his wife. He returned a moment later, looking quite puzzled.

"Tut! Tut! Tut!" the Gnome quirked anxiously about.

"What are you looking for now, fool?" asked his wife quite impatiently. "Your tutting is making me nervous."

'It's making me nervous too,' thought Mary Ann secretly for she dare not say it out loud for fear of making things even worse so.

"Tut! Tut! If I knew what I was looking for then I wouldn't hardly have lost it, now would I? Now, if I only could remember what it was I was looking for..."

His wife just simply shook her head, and muttered under her breath, "I'll tell you what you've lost, old fool, you've lost your mind for good!"

"Oh, here it is!" the Gnome exclaimed, proudly holding up an old rusted saw.

"Well, what on earth do you need THAT for?" the wife muttered again, this time more audibly.

"Oh dear, now that's a bother. I forget what it was I was going to do." Slowly now, to himself he continued, "A saw... Now if I were a saw, what would I be doing?"

"A saw can be used for many things," began Mary Ann. "Usually to cut things down or make them smaller."

"Cut down. I could cut things down with a saw... No, that's not it. I could make things smaller with a saw... That's not it, either. What else is a saw good for?"

Mary Ann shrugged. "Some people know how to play the saw. As a musical instrument. I don't suppose you know how to play the saw, though. It's awfully rare."

"Silly girl, you're much too literal," the Gnome's Wife spoke, then to her husband continued, "The saw you found to remind you to see. It's your glasses you're looking for, dear, and they're on top of your head."

The Gnome reached up to the top of his head, fitting his spectacles smartly on his face.

"A-ha! There you are! Been wondering why I can't see clearly all day! From now on, remind me to get more glasses. I need to keep a pair in every room, just in case I lose one."

The Gnome's Wife answered, "You do have a pair in every room, you ol' goat... but I'll remind you just the same."

The two exchanged a sweet kiss.

Mary Ann just shook her head, confused as often enough, but happy that the Gnome had at least found what he was looking for and was now seated comfortably in his recliner, finishing his crossword puzzle.

CHAPTER SIX: PULL OF THE MOON

Standing in the doorway of the log cabin, Mary Ann scratched her head, no less confused than she'd been when she'd arrived (though less hungry).

"I can't seem to recall where it was that I was going now…"

"Yes, well that IS a problem," the Gnome's Wife said matter-of-factly.

Mary Ann continued, "That tea seems to have quite gone to my head. I feel funnily drippy suddenly..."

"It can do that," the Gnome's Wife said matter-of-factly.

Finishing now her thought, Mary Ann added, "It is, though, isn't it? Funny, I mean... a person not knowing which way they're going. That is to say... What would I have been strolling off in the middle of NOWHERE for? What on earth is the point of THAT?" She shivered just then. "My, but it IS rather chilly, isn't it? Rather looks like rain."

The Gnome's Wife hustled off in a tizzy. "Now, don't you go anywhere just yet, young lady," she warned with a flick of her finger.

This left Mary Ann and the Gnome, one as perplexed as the other, scratching their heads.

"Tut! Tut! I do wish we could help you more, but I mustn't stray too far from the cabin. The dogs, you know."

The dogs that the Gnome was referring to were, of course, two of the straggliest, mangiest mutts Mary Ann had ever laid eyes on. But then it stands to good reason that anything loved the way those dogs were must certainly be beautiful, which is to say that really ANYthing could be beautiful to SOMEbody if they just looked at it right.

Returning with a knitted cape, the Gnome's Wife threw it 'round Mary Ann's shoulders saying, "Now then, this will keep you warm from that chill you keep on about."

The Gnome shrugged. "I don't see where it's cold. Tut! Feels warm to me..."

His wife gave him a knowing stare.

He shrugged again, then called the dogs, "Angel, come! You too, HC. Come say 'So long!' to our visitor guest. Oh, Come on now... Don't just sit there... Come!"

The dogs, curled up close to the fire, just stared at him lazily (not all that different a stare as his wife had just given him, Mary Ann thought to herself). One rolled over onto its back and stretched its paws wide into the air before joining the Gnome by his side.

"Gooooood dog, Angel!" the Gnome congratulated, petting her mane furiously. "Such a good Angel, yes you are... My Angel girl..." Then looking up at the other dog, still lying there, added, "Now get up, H.C.! Do you hear me? Don't pretend like you can't hear me, you ol' ragamuffin! Tut! Tut! Come and say 'So long!'"

But the dog didn't budge, but went from staring to yawning to laying its head back down towards the fire, pretending to not have heard the Gnome quite at all in the first place.

Mary Ann was just thinking how very rude this was, when the Gnome began tutting quite uncontrollably now. (It should be noted that to 'tut' means to fret most generously. It can also be translated as 'flying monkey', but why, that clearly would make no sense whatsoever for purposes here, so we shall deduce that it was in the Gnome's habit then to fret.)

"H.C. COME!" the Gnome's Wife barked and the dog then stood and languidly sashayed to the seeing-off party.

'I must say,' Mary Ann thought to herself, 'that dog does ever-so much prefer the wife over the Gnome... But then, I suppose, I might, too, with all that tutting. Then again, if I were a dog, I might respond well to anyone who feeds me. The Gnome's Wife must feed her. Yes, that must be the case.' Mary Ann nodded in agreement with the thought, quite proud that she'd been able to follow that logic through. Thinking had, after all, become somewhat exasperated suddenly, and it was rather difficult to hold one straight for longer than 3.14 seconds.

"Tut! Tut!" the Gnome shook his head disapprovingly at the dog. But the old mutt disregarded his reproach, walking straight toward Mary Ann, head held low.

She bent down to rub behind its hind quarters and with tail wagging, the dog plopped down squarely on top of her feet.

"Well, if I didn't know any better, I'd say she was sad to see you go," the Gnome's Wife noted.

"That true, then?" Mary Ann queried the dog. "Are you trying to keep me here?" H.C. looked up at her longingly then licked her nose.

And then the strangest thing happened. From somewhere deep inside Mary Ann's brain came a kind of screaming pressure as if her face was quite about to burst.

"Would it be very strange of me to say that there seems to be a boiling teapot inside my head?" she asked aloud.

"A boiling WHAT?!" the Gnome replied, holding his ear toward her. "Hearing's going, I'm afraid. Tut! Tut! Can't quite make out words the way I used to. Tut! Could've sworn you said 'boiling tea.' Is that correct?"

The wind stirred brewfully.

"Yes," she went on to explain, "I know it sounds quite odd when I say it out loud like that, but it feels like a tea kettle is about to go off inside."

She was just about to lose that train of thought (for it had been already been over 3.14 seconds), when from the cabin came the sound of a whistling kettle, presumably for more tea.

"Well, that IS an odd coincidence, indeed!" the Gnome's Wife remarked, stealthily backing away. "Going to go turn down the heat, then..." she continued, walking slowly backwards toward the cabin, eyes fixed on Mary Ann.

The Gnome surveyed her curiously. "Tut! How'd you know that kettle was about to go off?"

"Well, I should hardly know HOW exactly. It wasn't like that..." she struggled for words then landed at: "It was just a sound that was heard before it happened. I happen to have excellent hearing!"

"A sound that was heard before it happened, eh? Tut! Why, that sounds funny," the Gnome pondered, combing his beard in hand.

"Sounds funny to you, does it? But it's hardly funny to me... Well, I mean... That is to say... Funny in a not so funny sort of way."

The Gnome grew decidedly more anxious.

"Oh dear... Stop now with all this funny business! Tut! All this rhyming... What shall we do?" With this, the Gnome peeked nervously inside the cabin doorway. "I'm not supposed to rhyme, you know... Wife doesn't like it when I do."

"Doesn't like it? Why-ever would anyone NOT like a rhyme?"

The Gnome shrugged. "Says it's enough the way I tut, must I talk nonsense in the hut, getting stuck in this rut makes her crazy in the kookoonut, she says but... But... But..."

Just then, the Gnome's Wife appeared in the doorway. She glared at him, face washed with a heavy coat of disappointment.

"Did I hear you rhyming just then? Is that what I heard, ol' fool, coming from your lips?"

The Gnome cowered, hunched shoulders turning his head to look in every which direction other than meeting the eyes of his wife, who was trying very hard to catch them with her own.

He tutted under his breath.

Mary Ann interjected with a genuinely decent question. "Why, don't you see that all your fussing about rhyming is upsetting him into a tuttling mess?"

The Gnome's Wife jolted in astonishment at the child's impertinent suggestion. "Who's fussing?" she remarked in short defense. "I'M not fussing! Surely no!" then to the Gnome continued, "Rhyme all you want, ya old nutter... See if I care!"

But before the Gnome could mutter a tut, Mary Ann interjected again, "Most excellent news, Gnome friends! I'm ever-so glad THAT got settled... Rhyming is really a sign of smarts, that's what Maemae Alice says. Why... Any tutter could conjure a clever sentence... but how many spin those words in rhyme to make the present tense?"

She cleared her throat for effect, then continued, "The Gnome is gifted to rhyme. You ought to be proud of that... It's very rare to find poets these days. They're something of an anomaly."

"Is that so?" the Gnome's Wife challenged.

"Indeed!" Mary Ann replied. "And such a rare thing as a poet who RHYMES most definitely so!"

The Gnome's Wife, "hmmphed!" in reply, then turned briskly back inside the hut without even so much as a "how d'you do" out.

Breaking the newly spelled tension between them, the Gnome spoke up then saying, "Suppose this is 'So long!' then." He wrapped her up in an awkward embrace adding, "So long, then," and returned inside himself, tutting all the way.

Mary Ann knelt down to pet the dog, consolingly.

"I dare say, it seems that I've somehow frightened the gnomes off. However it's possible for me to frighten I shan't know... My, but your face is funny, dog. So soft and flowy... I shall miss you too, you know." With this, the dog cocked his head. She continued, "But I promise you this: I won't forget you, dog."

And much to her surprise, the dog answered back, "Promise?"

So shocked was she by this that she lost her balance entirely, spilling onto the ground in a heap.

"Why, a talking DOG? In ENGLISH, no less! How fantastic!"

The dog scratched its ear with a scrawny hind leg. "Really? Fantastic, you say..."

"Well, I should think SO," stammered Mary Ann. "That dogs or cats should talk at all is something quite extraordinary, I should think! But when animals speak English... Why now, that's perfectly wonnnnnderful."

"English ist hässlich, nein?" H.C. proposed.
[English is ugly, no?]

"Oh my... I dare say you must have a cold, poor thing," Mary Ann answered, uncomprehending.

"Sprechen Sie Deutsch, kleines Mädchen?" H.C. retried.
[Do you speak German, little girl?]

Mary Ann rubbed the dog's chin.

"I'm awfully sorry, dog, but I've absolutely no idea what it is that you're trying to say. Now if it was French, then, perhaps... for I studied a bit of French in school. But whatever it is that you were saying just then is lost entirely. Do you speak French, then?"

H.C. sighed. "Mitleid... und nein."
[Pity... and no.]

Mary Ann paused from scratching H.C.'s ear. "I really must insist on English. Not understanding the characters in my own story is absolutely unacceptable henceforth!"

H.C. tossed a wet lick to her ear. "I shall miss you, m'lady. It was ever so nice to make your brief acquaintance. And I wish you Godspeed."

"Oh, why THANK YOU, dog! Thank you ever-so much," and then that very brief thought got interrupted by another one that suggested that it was German that the dog was speaking. This rather made sense, since it was a sort of German Shepherd-looking scrappy mutt of a dog. Realizing this, of course, did her no good for she didn't speak German and it only served to lose her place in the conversation quite entirely. The dog nuzzled its nose under her arm for one final pet and looked into her faraway eyes lovingly.

"Auf Wiedersehen, schöner," H.C. said sadly then.
[Good-bye, beauty.]

Mary Ann gave the dog a squeeze topped off by a peck to the head.

"Good-bye, my friend. Now be a good dog and listen to your master. He is ever-so good a master to have, you know."

With this, the dog bowed its head low. Mary Ann stood then, surveying the scene, absolutely at a loss for where to begin. It seemed from someplace deep inside her that she'd seen this all before... not this place, mind you... for there really was not much of anything to see but an empty expanse of desert stretched out before her. It was a feeling more than anything, really. A feeling like she'd seen this all before in not-knowingness... an almost sort of lost sensation, quite discomforting.

Just then, as she breathed in, the air 'round her shifted and the day suddenly turned to night. Shed illumination long gone from the horizon, the air grew colder, and Mary Ann tucked the cape round herself tightly.

In dimly lit passage, she bore unawares in an easterly direction.

The dog's compassionate gaze followed her as she went.

"Frieden" was all it said.
[Peace]

Above in the sky, an ominous moon blazed glaringly. It has often been said that if you look closely at the moon on the full moon cycle, you can see a face there. This night was no exception.

Tonight the face of the moon was that of a screaming woman.

CHAPTER SEVEN: TAROT 18 INSIDE THE LOOKING-GLASS

Due to her recent apparent amber tea-induced amnesia, Mary Ann had quite also forgotten all about the wishing power granted her as a human being in a make-believe world. This in addition then to having lost the Sword of Truth and being, well, lost in every other sort of way, she stumbled on into the night, hazily dragging her feet, feeling dreadfully miserable when a tiny whisper buzzed, "She's had a bit of that amber tea, hasn't she?"

Mary Ann twisted 'round to see who it was speaking... first to the right, then the left, but either which way she looked, there was no body to match the sound.

'Of course,' thought Mary Ann, 'It is an awfully small sound, indeed... perhaps I ought to check under my feet to make certain I haven't injured another small-sounding friend as I did before. Oh, dearest me! Whatever WAS his name? Fiddlesticks on haystacks, I can't seem to recall a thing!'

"She's not thinking steady," the frail voice continued. "It's because she drank that amber tea, I tell you."

"So what if I have?" Mary Ann answered to the air. "What's it to you? And who are you, anyway? Why don't you show yourself to me if you know so much?" She bundled her hands into fists and put on a brave face. "Afraid of me, are you?"

A tiny laugh broke out. "Tee hee hee. She thinks she's frightening! How solidly delightful!"

Mary Ann swooped low, just missing the curiously swift swath of vrrrrroooming past her ear.

"I say! Show yourself, then... if you aren't so frightened."

"Tee hee hee. But I am showing myself, kiddo. Can't she see me?"

She looked about, glancing up and down, side to side, before stating quite vehemently, "Now see here... I am off on an important sort of journey and there is no time to waste fooling around with invisible sorts of characters."

The frail voice stiffened. "Important, she says. Why then, I should think I'll make an excellent traveling companion. I do well with important things."

By now, Mary Ann had grown very tense, indeed. "How am I to know if you're friend or foe, if I can't even see you?"

"That I do not know," the frail voice said. "Nor do I know how it is that she's not

88

quite blind. Tee hee." A quick clearing of the small throat then, "It's hard to miss me. I am, after all, a dragon."

"A DRAGON?!?" Mary Ann quizzed, befuddled. "However could a dragon be carrying around such a slight pitch?"

"Because," answered the voice wafting now directly before her eyes, "I am a dragonFLY."

And so it was. A red swarthy-tipped winged creature that looked very much the same as any ordinary fly except it had the body of a miniature dragon.

"Can she see me now?" it said.

Mary Ann marveled. "Why yes, I can... I can see you." Blinking, she continued, "But you're so... small. For a dragon, I mean."

"Small?" The dragonfly pulled back, looking offended. "However do you mean 'small'? I'm not small, I'm FEROCIOUS!" With that, it buzzed through the air in front of her, swooshing this way and that. "And powerful!" Now tumbling into a corkscrew of a tailspin, then swooshing back up to finish, "And would she like to see me breathe fire? Huh? Would she? It's pretty smart..."

Locked in a trance of dizzying dragon-talk and spontaneous swooshing (and partially still groggy from the amber tea), Mary Ann could muster only a nod.

"Hold out her hand, then," the dragonfly ordered.

There upon her hand, the dragonfly crooned in for a soft landing. After a series of complicated leg and wing stretches, the dragonfly stood at attention. Poised for action, he cleared his throat. Mary Ann focused, attentively. He cleared his throat again. Poised. Then burst forth into another round of stretches.

"Oh, DO come on! I haven't got all day!"

The dragonfly held forth a talon, signaling 'just one moment please', then drawing a deep breath, held it for what seemed like... well, definitely longer than 3.14 seconds because by the time the fire breathing was started, Mary Ann had quite moved onto another thought and missed it entirely, her focus distracted by her sore feet.

The dragonfly threw his wings up in the air, exasperated. "She missed it! Great. That's just great. Don't mind me... I'm just a dragon, ya know. It's not like I just breathed fire or anything.! Nothing really special about that, ya know."

"Ever-so sorry," she began, "It's just these shoes. They're terribly uncomfortable to walk in. The heel on them is far too much to manage..."

"Maybe she should try taking the heels off then," the dragonfly suggested. "An important journey requires a decent pair of comfortable shoes, ya know. Did she want to see me do it again? The fire-breathing, I mean."

Mary Ann answered, "Yes, please," busily slamming her patent leather shoes against the hard earth, smashing the heels off, as directed.

"Did she want to watch then while I do it?"

She adjusted her focus back to the dragonfly and patiently waited, trying very hard not to be rude. Clearing his throat once more, the dragonfly heaved a miniature yet potent flame, which very nearly singed the hem of her cape.

Mary Ann gasped, "Why, that is ever-so impressive, I must say!"

The dragonfly bowed. "Thank she."

"Ferocious friend, it is very good to know you. You shall make a most excellent traveling companion. Where then shall we go? Which direction do YOU suppose is best?"

"Why doesn't she try spinning around and wheresoever she stops, then that should be the direction of importance. For a journey of importance, this is often the way to find proper direction," the dragonfly offered.

"What an excellently clever suggestion!"

The dragonfly replied simply, "It happens."

So she spun around and around and feeling quite dizzy from spinning so, fell to the ground in a heap. Having landed smartly on her vine-veined arm, Mary Ann took one look at the purple bruise creeping its way onto her forearm and broke down in tears.

"I wish I knew what was really going on here," she sobbed.

And no sooner had the words escaped her lips, then she was swept up in the eye of a bursting tornado wind, the dragonfly following directly after her... Swooshing up and up and UP! Swiftly past the screaming face of the full moon and further on... Up, up, and away.

Just as she was beginning to enjoy the swooshiness of what seemed very much to her like flying, Mary Ann was dropped hard into a circular room walled in with looking-glass. It was, on second thought, more like one long, continuous looking-glass globe of a sort that she and the dragonfly had landed themselves in.

A glance any which way was decidedly unpleasant, for Mary Ann was not in the least bit pleased with the look of herself in the reflections she saw. Wrecked patent leather shoes with the heels knocked off, her once-fancy blue dress in tatters with ribbons flopping all about and delicate lace trim ripped, bruised arms ensconced in vine veins that bulged beneath her singed velvet cape. Besides the obvious costume disaster, her body had grown fat and her face quite mean, and overall Mary Ann thought, she had turned into the very ugliest little girl there ever had been.

"Why there you are, you sneaky little tart!" cried the voice of the Littlest Princess. "I've been looking all over for you..."

She sat reclined on a giant pink rocking unicorn (quite like rocking HORSE except for the unicorn HORN part on its head). The Littlest Princess teeter-tottered gleefully on the rocking unicorn, admiring her imaginary magic wand.

"I went off to fetch you a Rainbow of Hope, but when I returned, you'd disappeared. As a princess, it's customary for subjects to do as I say. Rudeness vexes me, you know. I am very. Put. Out," she pronounced, turning her gaze angrily toward Mary Ann.

The Littlest Princess took a moment to collect herself. She then stated all too calmly, "What. Are. You. Doing... WITH MY RED HAIR!" and with that, she added emphasis with a stomp so furious, it shook the entire globe.

"I say!" Mary Ann answered unwaveringly, "I shan't think it to be YOUR red hair any more than it is mine."

"Yes it is! YES IT IS!" the Littlest Princess tantrumed. Collecting herself again, she continued, "It is my red hair, because I am the only one who has it. I am the only one allowed to have red hair because I am the fiercest."

"Who says you're the fiercest?" Mary Ann queried, challengingly. "I haven't seen one lick of fierceness from you. All I've seen is nothing but a spoiled little brat with minions she likes to order 'round and control and who chokes beautiful flowers just for being more beautiful than she is. I look at you and see nothing more than a dress-up doll with a temper. That doesn't make you fierce, Princess, it only makes you MEAN."

"And what would YOU know about mean, huh?" came an alarming voice from behind. Mary Ann turned and there stood the Ringmaster, looking quite fierce himself, in a violent sort of fierce way.

"Think you could just shut me up, eh?" quoth the Ringmaster. "Is that what you thought, you impudent, fat, ugly child!" Catching her sheer panic stare, he added, "What, now you think I'm crazy, huh? Is THAT what you're thinking? HA!"

"If anyone 'round here's crazy it's got to be that... that... that..." came another angry-toned snap from her other side.

Mary Ann switched her gaze to the left to find the dreaded Troll basking at the feet of the Littlest Princess, being fanned quite puppet-like by her imaginary magic wand.

"That once pretty thing left me! After how I cared for her after that awful witch's stench!" To this very last point, the Littlest Princess nodded in agreement.

"EEP! Eep eep eep? Eeeeep!"

Professor Firefly careened in for a landing on the Littlest Princess' shoulder.

"Killed you THREE TIMES, did she?" the Littlest Princess translated. "My, oh my... Three times!"

Professor Firefly gasped.

The Princess continued, "Yes, she does have a way of leaving without even so much as a good-bye. Poof! Gone. No farewells or anything!" Pausing to shift her attention from Professor Firefly to Mary Ann, she continued, "Unduly RUDE and ridiculously unconscionable!"

Greatly stung by the sadness of this last betrayal, Mary Ann offered, "Come now, Professor... It wasn't three times that I killed you. Only the once and that was quite on accident. The second time, well that was HIS fault," she said pointing toward the Ringmaster. "And there wasn't a third time at all, for by the second... And I DO apologize for never farewelling, but I thought you very much in danger so I did a quite sensible thing in wishing you away before anything more dastardly should happen to you. I cared for you, Professor, you simply MUST believe me!"

Professor Firefly meekly eeped in reply.

"What I want to know,' began an eerily-seductive drone from behind the looking-glass, "Is what did you think you were doing by stealing my riddle, Alice?"

Mary Ann turned to face the formless Fool, her voice quivering in reply, "I did nothing of the sort! I was simply trying to solve it for you."

"WHO SAID I WANTED IT SOLVED?" boomed the Hatter Fool from beyond.

"Why, I should think that would be the point of a riddle, isn't it? To be solved, I mean." She tried in earnest not to shudder in fear. To little avail.

"You stupid girl," chimed in the Troll. "You really think a riddle is for being SOLVED?" And with this, the Littlest Princess and Professor Firefly burst into a fit of laughter.

Mary Ann herself burst in an entirely different sort of way, for the painful jabbing of all of that cruel laughter made what was left of her poor splintered heart crumble into dust. And so it was that she burst once again into a fit of crying.

The sight of all this enraged her new friend, the ferocious dragonfly so... That sweeping courageously close to the looking-glass in front of her, he drew the deepest breath he could muster. A blast of fiery righteousness ushered forth, unfolding the looking-glass (much like the pages of this book) to reveal her bedroom at home, just on the other side of the reflection.

The dragonfly fell, life force drained quite completely from his frail body.

"Now look what you've done!" the Hatter Fool scolded.

"But I haven't done anyth–" Mary Ann began, the words suddenly catching in her throat. Her attention decidedly diverted by the image before her from beyond the other Side.

For behind the looking-glass wall, inside the bed that seemed ever-so familiar in a bedroom that looked very much like her own at home, was nestled a little girl who had a semblance quite likened to her own. Sleeping soundly as you please.

"What is happening here?" she felt her mouth say. Then raising a horrified hand to her mouth to cover the next thought aloud, "What have I done?"

The Hatter Fool stepped then in front of her reflection and taking a teacup from beneath his poppy-cocked hat, uttered disdainfully, "What have you, INDEED..."

CHAPTER EIGHT: TRAIN OF THOUGHTS

The pain from hearing the Fool speak so accusingly tormented the poor child so that she screamed at the top of her lungs between fitful sobs, "LEAVE ME ALONE! ALL OF YOU!" Then pausing briefly to sob some more, her face twisted in vexation, "I CAN'T HANDLE ANYMORE, I TELL YOU! I JUST WISH TO BE LEFT ALONE INSIDE MY OWN HEAD!"

And just like that, she found herself quite lifted from the horror of the Looking-Glass Globe into an empty box car on a stopped train, positioned upon the edge of a cliff.

Poking her head out of the box car window, Mary Ann looked down over the cliff's edge and blinking twice, noticed that it seemed to go on and on without end, much like the black holes she'd studied last semester in school. Glancing up then and 'round, her eyes followed the railroad tracks of the stopped train and noticed they were laid just along the perimeter of the bottomless pit.

Wiping tears from her sobby little head, Mary Ann noted grumpily, "Whoever would build a train that doesn't go anywhere but 'round and 'round? Why, no wonder it doesn't have any passengers! Who in their right mind would want to travel 'round in circles?"

Stepping out from the box car, she walked to the front of the train, peeking into each window for some trace of a body or face or anything at all.

"Hello? Anybody there?" Seeing no one, she added, "GOOD! This is ever-so much better... I don't need ANYBODY, I don't! I can quite manage all on my own, thank you very much, indeed!" With that, she plopped down, suddenly bored or exhausted (hard to say which) and muttered rather solemnly, "That's right, then. I did ask to be left alone, but I say... Left alone in the middle of the desert on a train going nowhere except 'round a black hole in the earth wasn't quite the thing I had in mind when I wished it."

An idea sprang to her mind just then. 'My heavens! How silly all that sobbing and going on has left me... All cloudy in the head again! I dare say, I'll just wish a new wish for someplace a good bit more agreeable than this ridiculous nonsense!'

(It should be noted that the place that Mary Ann had chosen to plop down was on the tracks directly in front of the train's bow, which obviously isn't at all a very clever place to land oneself. However, being alone on an empty train of one's own thoughts can be quite befuddling. Even for an Alice.)

Mary Ann evened her breath and having learned from her wishing mistakes prior, made an ever-so conscious effort to focus her attention this time before getting the wishing underway. To her surprise, the focusing game was far more possible than she'd imagined, for the effects of the amber tea had since worn off and the evening of her breath proved useful in clearing the air. Not only was it possible to hold a thought for longer than 3.14 seconds, but she felt quite astounded by the number of positively lovely options for excellent wishes that came to her, despite the wretchedly horrible things she'd just seen in the Looking-Glass Globe. Each time she thought up a new excellent wish, it seemed to double from 1 to 2 to 4 to 8 to 16 to 32 and so on and so forth until they seemed quite endless in number.

'For one,' she thought, 'when I find an ever-so much more pleasant spot to be in, I'll most assuredly wish for better friends than that two-faced Nothing Fool. Turn-coat that he is. To think that I'd steal his silly little riddle! Why, the thought of it makes me laugh! HA! HA!' and this rather unhappy thought rolled itself into a fit of very unhappy sounding laughter.

Just then, the wind shifted and the sky grew red. Storming clouds thundered in the distance and lightning flashed across the far horizon. Mary Ann felt every bit of the stinging weather coursing through her vine veins leading through to her dust-splintered murmuring heart.

BA DUM. BA DA DUM. DA DIPPITY DUM DA DUM.

DA DUM. BA DA DUM. DIPITY DIPPITY DUM.

Head pulsing with brain shock, her vine vein arms now undulating with a eerie snake-like fervor that quite reminded her of the hideous green black serpent from before. All of this creepiness only served to volley her memory once more to the Nothing Fool and their cherished lost waltz. This last thought shut down her laughter altogether and from somewhere more bottomless than the pit before her, she let go the very saddest cry that ever was uttered at the top of a sad person's lungs: "I... WISH... TO... BE... HOME!!!"

She waited for a change.

But there was none.

None.

No change whatsoever. Still in the distance, the storm clouds increased and red wind picked up pace, causing her dust-splintered heart to quicken its' unsteady pounding.

BA DA DIPPITY DUM. DA DIPPITY DUM. DIPPITY DUM.

DIPPITY DUM DA DIPPITY.

So she repeated, more loudly this time, "I WISH TO BE HOME!"

...

...

...

Nothing, but the threatening sound now of the dreaded marching towers now approaching from the westerly direction. This was enough to send Mary Ann reeling in horror.

"Fine, then! I don't need any more of you, silly wishes!"

The marching towers traced closer, edging Mary Ann's mind with sharpest intensity. She shouted courageously to the towers marching, "AND I SHAN'T NEED YOU, EITHER!" - to which the sound of the marching towers stopped.

Mary Ann, now feeling very much like the broken pieces of her poor tattered heart, whispered an almost indiscernible plea, "What difference does it make, anyway?" Then bravely lifting her voice angrily but firmly to no one in particular continued, "Everybody either hates me or tries to fix me. Well, I don't need to be fixed! DO YOU HEAR ME? I DON'T NEED TO BE FIXED!"

Softening now, she added, "No one there to hear me. Nobody ever does, it seems. Whatever shall I do since the wishing won't work and this silly train certainly isn't going to get me anywhere and the weather is ever-so foreboding to travel anywhere away. I suppose my only other option since I can't go on or out from here is to go... In."

She rose to her feet in a single elegant swoop and walked with baby steps to the very edge of the cliff. Looking down into the bottomless pit, she remembered falling through formless darkness before and considering that it hadn't been quite as awful as all this out HERE, decided resolutely that her choice was a good one, indeed. She summoned courage from inside the belly of the unrisen sun and facing the bottomless pit, steadied herself to leap.

Drawing a deep breath, Mary Ann shut her eyes and opened her arms wide as she plunged into the abyss. Her body tumbling 'round from the thrust of her fall, she opened her eyes toward the deep blue sky hanging like a canopy of stars. The last thing to catch her attention before the ground above vanished from view was the front of the train with a curious destination marker that read: LOCO MOTIVE.

Now deep inside the abyss, the little girl reached instinctively out from the darkness to grab hold of a lotus flower that suddenly appeared just in time for her to grasp it. Burying her face into the flower's flesh, she felt the center stretch forward and tap-tap-tap on her forehead on the space directly between her eyes. A picturesque pattern of kaleidoscope colors swept her focus so that it wrapped the ever-changing tessellation into one encompassing, limitless hue.

"Here we go!" she felt her lips say.

Into the Color of Oneness she flew... Soaring neither up nor down nor in nor out nor conceivable of any direction in any plane she'd ever known before. The warmth of the lotus' kiss now enveloping with sweetest Serenity, she surrendered to the Everything held inside the great Nothing. And just...

Let...

Go.

CHAPTER NINE: THE HOLY COUNCIL

When she opened her eyes, she was standing in a crystal cathedral, surrounded by thrones of platinumest gold.

A Voice from one of the thrones announced, "Welcome to Lynnfinity!" then bowed its head continuing, "Aaaaaaaa..." in a low sustained chant. The Voice belonged to what Mary Ann presumed to be a sort of elephant man with the most marvelous demeanor held seemingly in perfect composition with six (for she counted them twice to be sure) mesmerizing arms waving in fluctous rhythm.

The thrones 'round about the elephant man hummed in harmonic chorus, "Aaaaaaaaaaahhh..."

"Well hello! How'd you do? Sorry to pop in like this, interrupting your... your... well, whatever this is! Majestic meeting of some kind... I really can't rightly say. Ever-so inviting though!" Mary Ann began, trying her best to be polite, as her mother had taught her. "Would any of you kind strangers happen to know where it is that I've happened along to now, then?"

A familiar face spoke next, "Welcome to Lynnfinity."

"Oh, hello Shaman! Fancy seeing you here!"

Shaman Ka bowed his head in reverence.

Mary Ann curtseyed.

"Why, thank you, good sir. But what's Lynnfinity? Or should I say... Where? For you see, there was a particular destination I was expecting to find... and I'm afraid, as enchanting as Lynnfinity is, this isn't it."

From two thrones over to the right of the Shaman Ka, a laugh bellowed from what looked very much to Mary Ann to be a book seated there on another throne.

'How very curious, indeed!' Mary Ann thought to herself.

Book said, "Lynnfinity is a limitless noun, a dimension of vibration that exists roughly between time and space."

"Oh, I see," Mary Ann offered, quite trying to comprehend. "But I think the word you're looking for is 'infinity'," (for she'd heard her mother refer often to the word in describing the level of her frustration with Mary Ann's constant rebellion). "Quite close, however. It IS such a pleasant sounding word, isn't it though?"

To this, Book stated plainly, "Words are my specialty. The word 'Lynnfinity' is in this case a correct one."

Seated between the Shaman Ka and Book was a figure of such presence that Mary Ann thought she looked very much like a queen. Upon the supposed queen's lap, sat two small children – one propped on each knee. Presuming a queen must surely be in charge, Mary Ann thought it smart to check her with the query, "Is that quite right?"

"Yes," was the reply. She then added kindly, "I am Akasha." Pointing to her right with a gesture of sheer elegance she continued, "Welcome to Holy Council."

"Yes, welcome," spoke a slightly bowed head who seemed to very much resemble Jesus. "I am called Tricky Buddha."

Mary Ann curtseyed again.

"I am Ganesha," boomed the elephant man with six arms.

"In Kenzo," quoth a green faerie gently, positioned just to the left of the Shaman Ka.

Surrounding the green faerie's throne, fluttered a garden of the most adorable child faeries who seemed to be dancing to music as quiet as they were tiny. Upon catching Mary Ann's stare, the child faeries giggled then took turns with coquettish bows.

[Here then is a diagram of the Holy Council for reference]

GANESHA

(empty seat)   TRICKY BUDDHA

MARY ANN

IN KENZO
BOOK

SHAMAN KA   AKASHA

"Of course you know who I am," spoke Shaman Ka.

"Oh yes," Mary Ann added, nodding pleasantly.

Shaman Ka beamed. "It pleases me to see you smile."

And so she smiled some more.

"Has anyone seen the Good Witch?" asked Queen Akasha.

In Kenzo replied, "She's off on an errand. Said it was of most urgent attention. I don't know --"

"-- If perhaps we should call her," continued Ganesha.

"We shall call her," the Tricky Buddha agreed.

In unison, the circle of thrones chanted again in perfect harmony, "Aaaaaaaaaaaaaahh..."

The tiny faeries joined in the sweet chorus, "Aaaaah... Ooooooo...." The voices from all thrones in perfect harmony singing, "Oooooooooooooh..."

Mary Ann, not understanding a lick of what was happening but quite liking it none-the-less, chimed in timidly, "Um..." to begin her innocent query into the current curious state of affairs.

The circling thrones bowed in humble astonishment. This confused Mary Ann all the more.

Ganesha raised his right hand, palm facing her. On it was tattooed a symbol that looked something like this:

Mary Ann thought it looked quite like a three with a broken question mark riding on its coattails. She was just thinking about how it could also be something like a broken heart with a hanging one-eyed smile, when suddenly-

"HERE!" popped in the Good Witch, now occupying the empty throne. As she did so, the chanting from Holy Council stopped. All heads about thrust themselves downward in enraptured exultation.

"We –" directly followed the voice of Shaman Ka.

"—Are!" finished Ganesha.

"Well, hello again! I know you..." Mary Ann said to the Good Witch, completely forgetting now her query. "You're that witch who threw me into the most stenchiest of spells!"

The Good Witch tossed her broom to the ground in noisy clatter, muttering to herself while looking at it, "Blasted old contraption! Out of juice again!"

Mary Ann tried once more, "I said, 'Hello'... You might do well to remember me, Good Witch. I was the doll, you know... The one who fainted from the Land of Lost Toys. You struck me with a horrible spell which made me follow that awful wretched Troll away from all my friends. Then I got lost, I'll have you know... And have been lost ever since, it seems... Trying to find my way. Do you remember me, then? Well, do you?"

The Good Witch straightened herself replying, "Of course I remember you, child. Though it wasn't me who made you follow the Troll away. You did that quite on your own accord, I'm afraid."

"But how can you say that?" Mary Ann retorted, looking about the Crystal Cathedral for some reassurance. "I was put under a spell, I was. A stinky, stupid, horrible spell cast by that... that..." she continued, pointing rudely, "That witch!"

"I agree," the Good Witch began, "That it wasn't the spell I had intended, but it served you even better in the end, it would seem. You are here in the most sacred of space, after all. So mote it be."

In Kenzo to the Good Witch's right agreed, "So mote it be."

"But whatever ARE you talking about?" Mary Ann shouted. "Better? Is that what you said just then? BETTER?"

The Shaman Ka nodded his head calmly, "Better."

Mary Ann quite liked the Shaman Ka so she decided to ask him then, "But how? How 'better'? I suppose you think that getting dragged all about going from this place to that, never knowing where at all it is that you're at and finding yourself all bloodied and bruised and cut up and spit out and yelled at by all sorts of so-called friends who quite obviously hate you... I suppose this is better, is it? Better than what is what I'd like to know!" And with that, she concluded finally with a dramatic shake of her head.

"Peace --" serenely spoke the Tricky Buddha.

The Good Witch picked it up from there continuing, "The intended spell was to be. But I mixed up my 'L' for the 'D' or rather, my 'D' for the 'L' - I really ought to get a spell check... Forever misspelling I am." She wagged a knowing finger at Mary Ann adding, "But always for the better. I assure you. Blessed be."

The tiny faeries agreed in small chorus, "Blessed be!"

"For love you wished," Mary Ann said, tears welling up in her eyes. "Love. Only I didn't get love... or a dove or anything of the sort. All I got was a boorish Troll slugging along beside me, then loneliness and confusion and quite a screaming dose of nonsense!"

"Make no mistake, child. The spell itself was right as rain. 'Twas I who blundered, but only in the methodology. You were given precisely what you needed most. And got most precisely the love you so desire."

"What love is that, then?" Mary Ann demanded.

The child Morgan seated atop Akasha's right knee answered, "The love --"

And the child Little Lizzie on the other completed the thought saying "-- Of wandering."

Mary Ann shook her head in disbelief thinking, 'Why, it makes no sense! How could someone love to wander?' Now, if it was WONDERing... then perhaps she could see the rationale in that. But wandering? Simply impossible! Ridiculous! And otherwise incomprehensible! And then, quite obviously... Wrong. 'Why, I haven't enjoyed wandering about even the slightest! It's been nothing but dreadful the entire time. Well, not the absolute ENTIRE time,' she remembered then (thinking of her first meeting with Professor Firefly and the endearingly enchanted lost waltz with the Nothing Fool). However even the really grand moments were ruined by something or other that seemed to always take her away to a worse predicament than the one before. Why, ever since she awoke in the reclining chair of that strange room with the Mochakie Cat, it had been nothing but an absolute nightmare!

Mary Ann was just about to mention this to the Holy Council when her train of thought was derailed by the Good Witch who gently explained, "Where do you think all that wishing came from? It came from your heart... Your very heart's desire made those things happen. Nothing more or less."

"But my poor heart is in shambles!"

103

The Good Witch smiled tenderly, cupping her face in hand, much like Miss Tulip's tender petal. "I know, child... I know." Then looking up and around the assembly of the Holy Council, she solemnly spoke, "But you are... Most obviously... Quite. Loved."

In Kenzo nodded in agreement, "Loved."

The Good Witch drew herself up and out of her throne. Carrying the Sword of Truth outstretched in front of her, she approached Mary Ann saying, "You were given all the tools you needed to make your journey complete."

Handed the Sword of Truth now, Mary Ann noted curiously that it weighed significantly lighter than it had been before.

"It would appear," the Good Witch began, "That the desire of your heart was to follow this wanderlust from wish to wish until all of those wishes brought you back to the beginning again."

The Holy Council assembly nodded reverently in accord.

Holding her head now not quite so proudly, Mary Ann said humbly (and almost too softly to hear), "I should think with all that's happened that I shan't be so bold as to ask for one last wish granted." Speaking louder then she added, "But I am and I shall."

"Clever girl," touted Ganesha, lovingly.

The Good Witch queried, "What wish is that, child?"

Mary Ann replied, "Why to go home, of course!"

Ganesha answered, "You carry your home with you everywhere you go."

Tricky Buddha added, "Your home --"

Akasha continued, "-- Is inside --"

"-- Your heart," In Kenzo completed the thought.

Looking down quizzically at her heart, Mary Ann stated with furrowed brow, "Well, I shan't think there's much room at all in there for my bedroom and things..."

The Good Witch giggled, "Ah! THAT home, you mean... I see." Then reaching a hand up underneath her witch's hat, brought forth a brass key which she then presented. "Take this, then. This should do it!"

Mary Ann took the key, but not knowing in the slightest what to do with it, decided to tuck it away inside her pocket for sake keeping.

"Now then, before you go... I simply must do something about this ridiculous get-up. Most unacceptable for an Alice of your stature," the Good Witch said. Then, pushing back her sleeves, she spread her arms open wide over Mary Ann's quite disheveled body with tangled red locks and tattered blue ribboned dress, and focusing intently this time, pronounced:

"A la snafoo
A la shazam
Make this child
Ratatatam

Song of the heavens
Welling above
Innocence carry
On wings of a DOVE"

And with that last (corrected) spell, Mary Ann was returned to her normal(ly disheveled) self again.

Then placing her hands over Mary Ann's, she lifted them up with the sword between them, high above her head, and announced to the ethers: "TRUTH."

Ganesha: "PROTECTION."

Tricky Buddha: "STRENGTH."

Book: "WISDOM."

Akasha: "COMPASSION."

Morgan and Little Lizzie in unison: "COURAGE."

Shaman Ka: "JOY."

In Kenzo: "LOVE."

Mary Ann's attention drifted from face to face, drawing in the echo surrounding her from the Crystal Cathedral into a deep inhale. Then steadily letting go her breath, she was instantly transported back to the Looking-Glass Globe once more.

*

Everyone was present. The Ringmaster, Troll, Littlest Princess, Professor

Firefly, and of course, the Hatter Fool. They were seated at a round table, playing a game of cards.

Surveying the scene, Mary Ann noticed the dragonfly lying listless on the floor by the now see-through looking-glass with her trapped Self on other side, resting unknowing, peacefully in her bed.

"All right," she announced, holding the Sword of Truth steadily in front of her, poised for battle. "LET'S END THIS, THEN!"

And a voice whispered from beyond, "What makes you think that anything ever ENDS?!"

CHAPTER TEN: SWORDS, PENS, RIDDLE RAVENS, AND SHILLINGS

"My! Glad you could join us!" the Hatter Fool decreed, proudly sipping a spot of tea.

"Glad indeed, Fool!" Mary Ann cried, approaching him then. "What have you done? Riddling me so with illusions and things..."

"Why, whatever do you mean, Alice?" replied the Hatter Fool, quite curiously. "And, I must ask you to sheath your..." he started, pointing to the Sword, "... Temper, if you please!"

Mary Ann shouted, "I do NOT please, Fool!" Then pointing to her trapped visage on the looking-glass's otherSide added, "Well, just LOOK at me!"

Just then, an image appeared in the doorway of the otherSide bedroom. An image so familiar that it made Mary Ann do a staunch double-take back and forth between sides of the Looking-Glass Globe.

It was the Nothing Fool himself... walking towards her otherSelf. "But, if THAT's the Nothing Fool, then what does that make YOU?" she poked the other Fool.

He sat down his teacup with care. Mary Ann noted, with peculiar sadness, that the teacup he had been using was none other the little one stolen by her dollies, now stolen again by this imposter.

She continued screaming in every which direction, "I say... Shoe is on the wrong foot! You've got it all mixed up... ALL OF YOU! Nothing but thieves and tricksters! I'm hardly the mean one around here, if you should very well ask me!"

"Well, I shan't ask you anything presently," offered the Hatter Fool, "For I must say, Alice, you seem quite MAD." Then turning to the players at the card table, added, "And not the least bit mad in the funny sort of way, you know." The players at the card table nodded, quite in agreement.

"So what if I am mad?" she further shouted. "What of it, then?"

"EEP! EEP!" gasped Professor Firefly.

Mary Ann turned her squared attention back to the otherSide of the Looking-Glass Globe, which seemed she thought inwardly ever-so dream-like. The Nothing Fool was stooped beside the bed, trying without luck to awaken the otherSide version of a sleeping Mary Ann.

She drew nearer to the Hatter Fool threateningly. "What DID you do, then?

Create a riddle of us for me to solve?" Pointing again to the dream-like visage beyond, "Is that what we are? Nothing but another one of your silly riddles to solve?"

The Hatter Fool raised one solitary finger in the air. "#1, You have managed the Nothing part right, Alice my dear, but that's about that." Raising a second finger and pointing them both in the direction of the looking-glass, "#2, That FOOL is no Hatter. I say, Alice! He's got quite a different hat on altogether. Not nearly ten shillings, six pence the craftsmanship as mine," he protested, fixing his own hat atop his head. "I should know, of course. I am a Hatter."

Mary Ann burst to retort, but the Hatter Fool stopped her short with the snap of his fingers in the air. "And #3, Once and for all, a riddle isn't always meant to be solved!" And with this, he bowed most dramatically.

The players at the card table applauded.

"Here! Here!" sang the Littlest Princess.

"Well said, sir!" went the Troll.

Now greatly perplexed and bubblingly anxious, Mary Ann scratched her head, peering through the otherSide. "Well, if I'm here... then that otherMe on the otherSide of the looking-glass must be me sleeping. But then, if THAT's the real world and this is all a dream, then how did the Nothing Fool get THERE?" She added now, directing her query to the Nothing Fool on the otherSide, "Is it REALLY you?"

The Hatter Fool popped his head into view. Then glancing back toward the scene behind the looking-glass answered directly, "Why, that's Nothing. Nothing At All!"

She turned her gaze back toward the Nothing Fool, now shaking her otherSide lithe body to awaken. But try as he might, his attempts to waken her failed. Distraught with concern, his head fell heavy... eyes drawing a perfectly aimed arc right through the veiled looking-glass... right into the very soul of a daft, little girl stuck inside a looking-glass globe. His eyes pleaded the words, which his lips formed silently from beyond, "Please... Come back."

Suddenly very anxious to greet the Nothing Fool with a big hearted hug, she surveyed the looking-glass between them. The wall was seamless, every which way her fingers traced along.

By now, the Nothing Fool stood – just on the otherSide – hands placed on the surface of the looking-glass... eyes following Mary Ann as she carefully sought for a crack or latch. Catching his stare, her hands met his, on opposite sides of the looking-glass. And though there was a whole world dividing them, it almost felt like they were holding hands. Almost.

Frustrated now, she faced the Nothing Fool and signaled for him to move back. Confused, he willingly obeyed. Then she raised the Sword of Truth high above her head, and just before she was ready to strike--

The Hatter Fool stepped forth to her and said, "Figuring it all out then, are we?" Then his eyes did the whirly twirl thing as before, and his body whirly twirled into Behold! The Mochakie Cat with the hat on his head, then continued congratulating his transformation quite boastfully, with whirly twirls to spare. He stopped then just before her, sneaking in a wink of his one unpatched eye, saying, "Well, it's about time SOMEBODY did!" With this final whirly twirl, he vanished into thin air with a swoosh and a grin, hat dropping to the floor.

Brushing away the Cat Hatter Fool gone up in smoke with a wave of her hand, Mary Ann declared, "Now then, really!" She glanced at the otherSide reflection continuing, "There's Nothing to figure out! This is MY story, after all... Thank you very much!"

Attention averted now to the task at hand, Mary Ann once again raised the Sword of Truth high overhead and with all of her might, drove the blade through the looking-glass wall in a single, clean thrust.

Sensibly, the Nothing Fool stepped through the slice into this present reality.

"Why hello, Alice," he waved, and then to the card table, tipping his hat, "How d'you do? How d'you do?" Walking straight over to the Hatter Fool's hat, the Nothing Fool dusted it off, removed his own, and fitting the new one cock-eyed on top of his head, decided aloud, "Ah, yes! Much better, indeed!"

A familiar Voice wafted through on the wings of a soft, cool breeze (that sounded, Mary Ann thought, ever-so much like the hum of the Holy Council chorus), "WRITE YOUR NAME, ALICE."

The Nothing Fool tapped the top of the Hatter Fool's hat. Just as he did so, his pupils turned to pools of whirly twirl waves, the edges of his mouth following suit, forming a wide grin. "I say, Alice... Did you ever get 'round to why a raven is like a writing desk?"

Mary Ann smirked. "I shan't know, Fool! Shall we consult them both then and see what THEY say?"

The Nothing Fool's face drew back in mock horror. "I say, Alice! Curiously clever idea, indeed!"

Sensibly, the Troll spoke up, "But neither are here."

"Ah yes, well... Your Highness, my dear, would you mind ever much?" asked the Nothing Fool to the Littlest Princess.

"Only if I may have a peek at your hand," she bargained, glancing at the Fool's cards on the table.

"Oh, pfffft!" replied the Nothing Fool with a flick of his go-ahead hand.

The Littlest Princess peeked then a good long gander, acknowledging the cards thus, "Mmm hmmm..." Then looking up, quite pleased as can be, tapped her imaginary wand into the air, drawing forth a writing desk right next to the Nothing Fool, on whom was also now a raven rest-nesting on his right shoulder.

The Nothing Fool advised with the raven secretly. Turning back to address Mary Ann and the others, he whispered, "She's a bit shy. All this pressure, you know." Then he turned back to the raven assuringly, "Why, it's nothing more than a question between good friends is all."

The Raven Morrigana sneaked her beak in his ear. The Nothing Fool listened quite intently for a minute or four, murmuring, "Uh-huh. Oh, I see... Uh-huh. Oh... Hmmm... Right then!" Looking up at Mary Ann, he stated resolutely with a shrug of his shoulders, "She said, 'Nevermore!'"

"Fine, then," Mary Ann snapped, walking to the writing desk. Tossing aside the foolishness she felt, she asked the desk directly, "What of it, then? Why is a raven like a writing desk?"

Mary Ann waited for a reply. None came.

She waited again.

And waited.

Finally, the pregnant silence was interrupted by the Ringmaster's impatient tapping foot.

"Fallen silent, have we?" Mary Ann chided sternly, looking down at the desk. Upon it sat a pen of platimunest gold and next to that, her tattered notebook from the lost and found pile.

"WRITE YOUR NAME, ALICE," spoke the Voice from before.

Mary Ann looked at the pen and then at the Sword. Letting go of the second, she picked up the pen and wrote her name upon a blank page.

110

And just like that...

Everything, including both sides of the looking-glass, the broken-down Train of Thoughts, log cabin, camp of Mystikal Misfits, and breathing fireplace too... the Island of Magical Me, KooKooKaChoo Canoe, and Mystery Funland- Don't Miss It! included, the Land of Lost Toys, and yes, even the chair that she'd sat on, still comfy, reclined, and still sound...

Every single one of the characters whom she'd visited therein down to the very last letter...

Even you, dear reader...

Were swept up directly onto the page.

Then seeing all that she needed to see, the little girl straightened herself, and bravely taking the written page in hand, began aloud, "Mary Ann was an unusual child, given to spells...

PART THREE: WAKING LIFE

we are the offspring
of God's imaginary playmates

CHAPTER ONE: BECOMING AN ALICE

By the time Mary Ann had finished her story, having called forth every character until all had been presently accounted for, a mighty tribe assembled, poised between pages in the great Looking-Glass Globe.

She paused momentarily in the telling of the tale to drink in the pleasured company of her fellow adventurers. The pregnant pause was snatched up by critiques cascading over the crowd. Cap'n Beard Barak felt pride for his part however slightly disappointed at how seemingly small it had been, his gal Jag and the rest of That Camp shockingly remarked that they hardly even placed; H.C., on the other hand, was quite beeindruckt mit die Intelligenz; everyone it seemed had a two pence worth of opinion for how it had all been written... even Tricky Buddha had a question or two about his lines.

"Now listen here, ALL of you!" she shouted, addressing the Wanderlust assembly. "This is MY story, you see... MINE to tell! And I believe I've done quite smartly with it. It's not ever-so easy to construct a linear plotline with the likes of characters like YOU! But if any of you think that you'd like to tell your OWN version of the story... Or any story for that matter... Then I think you should. Tell it YOUR way in YOUR OWN story!" And with this, she dramatically curtseyed.

Owl courageously stammered, "I TH-TH-THINK W-W-W-WE SH-SHALL!"

The Gnome simply tutted at the suggestion.

"Good!" Mary Ann countered, confidently. "I say... The more storytelling, the better! But let the stories be told how YOU want it told, not the way some stuffed shirt grown-up is going to want it read. And for heaven's sake, don't drop your Sword of Truth like I did, prancing about distracted by things... You REALLY MUST focus!" She leaned in towards the crowd then, like a street corner evangelist ready to pitch a sermon, "Why, I'll bet that every last one of you could tell your own story a hundred time's better than I did... If you really put your mind to it!"

The Ringmaster turned privately to the Troll, "Is she for real or what?"

Mary Ann leaned her ear toward the Ringmaster. "Ever-so sorry... Didn't quite catch that. Were you asking if I'm for real or not?"

The Ringmaster nodded, doubtfully.

"Ah... Excellent question!"

After a short round of consecutive requests surrounding the repetition of the question at hand (for the characters in the very back couldn't hear), Mary Ann repeated loudly, "SOME OF YOU MAY BE WONDERING IF I'M FOR REAL OR NOT..."

The crowd fell deadly silent.

"WELL, WHAT DO YOU THINK?"

Not a peep.

Mary Ann softened. "You know, there is never an end to the number of questions that pop into the curious mind of an Alice. The mathematics for such a computation are far too advanced for my studies thus far, anyway. For seven highly improbable things before brunch leaves ever-so little time for rest-of-the-day imagining!"

"So if you're imagining all the time, then what are we, then... Just make-believe characters in your story, I suppose! HA! HAAAA!" Cap'n Beard Barak boomed. That Camp joined him in rip roaring laughter.

"Of course," she smiled lovingly at the assembly. Then spreading her arms out wide... Wide enough she imagined, to encompass every continent and every sea... from the slightest whisper of a decomposing cell to the noble eagle flying free on a whisper of the wind. Within the space between her two little arms stretched as far out as they possibly would go, Mary Ann squeezed it all into a big bear hug... Around the circumference of her own fragile, little heart.

"My name is Mary Ann. I am an Alice in a long line of Alices who've been mused and bemused the most magical of imaginary lands. If it weren't for the Alices, I should scarcely think this world would continue to exist... what, with people constantly bludgeoning one another with atrocious judgments over what's normal or proper... As if there is such a thing! Mother always goes on about how important it is to be a lady, poised and polite, but isn't it ever-so much more fun and wildly entertaining to be onto other bits... like building fairy tales just for fun? I think that's quite a clever way to pass the time amidst this otherwise boring evolution in the so-called REAL world!"

The crowd of characters murmured in agreement, "Mah-na mah-na phenomenanah...!"

The Littlest Princess stepped forward and presented with some smugness, her imaginary magic wand.

And with a flutter of her eyelashes, the Littlest Princess' imaginary magic wand turned quite not imaginary at all! Taking the now visible (and quite sparkly pink) wand in hand, the Littlest Princess tapped the air brightly with perfect intent. Out from nowhere popped Miss Tulip.

Miss Tulip addressed Mary Ann as well as the assembly in saying, "I hereby declare the most perfect imagination of this child set free in the crowning of Her Majesty Mary Ann as AN ALICE!"

"Mah-na Mah-na!" went the crowd in raucous accord.

Stepping down from the theatre of applause, Mary Ann slipped quietly out the back door. So caught up in rejoicing were the characters, not one noticed that she'd gone.

CHAPTER TWO: FREEDOM

Finding herself once again in the Foyer of Doors, Mary Ann inspected each and every one. She found each door locked, save one which stood slightly ajar... a flickering light invitingly beckoning from beyond.

Knowing quite well what was behind THAT door already, Mary Ann took the key the Good Witch had given her from inside her pocket. Carefully surveying the options of all the OTHER doors and quite confused on which to choose, she remembered with sad fondness the poor dragonfly and his advice on matters pertinent to finding direction on a Journey of Great Importance.

So she spun herself 'round and 'round until quite dizzy, then opening her eyes, walked straight (or, rather, wibbly-wobbly, for she felt ever-so tibbly-tobbly) toward the door directly in front of her.

Placing the key in the lock, it clicked! then turned. Then just as she was about to step through, she heard a "Pssst!" coming from behind the slightly ajar door on the other side.

It was the Nothing Fool, peeking there, grinning from ear to ear. "Stealing away without even a good-bye?"

"I can't go back, Fool," Mary Ann said solemnly. "Though I will miss you so... I must find my own way now."

Nothing Fool stood then, retorting smartly as you please, "Find your own way? But where?"

"To the next adventure, of course! But I kept the door open for us to find one another if we should ever get stuck on the path amidst Stuff N Things."

The Nothing Fool's grin was kissed with a single teardrop rolling down his cheek.

"Clever girl... What am I to do now?"

Mary Ann replied simply, "Why, Nothing! Nothing at all!"

Nothing Fool's sadness crushed into a laugh. Then from behind him, Wolf popped his head out from the doorway, then Daisy Red Rider, the Gnome and his wife, followed by the Prankster Pricken Chicken himself and Bob with the 404 too, and Cap'n Beard Barak and his gal Jag and the whole crew of the infamous Merry Band of Thieves.

"We're free!" cried the Gnome with his Wife by his side.

"You freed us, Alice!" Wolf agreed.

"Now nothing is impossible is nothing now!" squealed Bob with the 404.

Mary Ann nodded, a smile blossoming wide.

"Her name's not Alice," corrected the Nothing Fool. "Though she is AN Alice, so I could see your confusion." He stepped toward her and in locking gaze added, "But only a Mary Ann could waltz with a riddle..." Outstretching his arms now in waltz dance position, he peeled a mischievous grin from within, "Give us one last dance, then."

"How could I ever possibly refuse a waltz with you?" she confessed. Walking toward him, she raised her arms to ready, but just before proceeding, suggested, "But this time YOU lead, Fool, for my heart is far too broken to keep a steady beat."

"Very well, then. I'm not quite used to leading but for you, I shall try." Then taking her in his arms, they waltzed 'round and 'round and 'round the Foyer of Doors.

"I say," chimed a resurrected Mochakie Cat, perched high above on the candle candelabra suspended mid-air. "A grand waltz! How very GOOD a thing to Doooo!"

And with this pronouncement, the Gnome and his Wife joined in the dance, as did Cap'n Beard Barak and his gal Jag, Wolf with the Troll, the Littlest Princess with the Ringmaster, and even Professor Firefly and Owl flew in on the trance.

They danced and danced, 'round and 'round, until finally her heart feeling so full she thought it might burst, Mary Ann squished the Nothing Fool in a hug just warm enough to melt back all the broken pieces of her tattered heart together again.

CHAPTER THREE: HOME

"Me-OW!" hissed the cat, being squeezed quite to death.

"Oh, my heavens!" her mother shrieked, entering the bedroom in a flurry.

"Why, Leoben! How I've missed you so!" Mary Ann said, addressing her cat lovingly, yet with some intensity. "You woke me out of quite a very strange dream, indeed! And you were there with me, all along through it, weren't you?"

With that, the cat pounced away, flouncing his orange tail in the bounciest of ways.

"I'm glad to see you decided to join the land of the living," scolded her mother. "You've been out cold for nearly the entire morning." Then clapping her hands briskly together added sternly, "Time to get up now and on with the day. Chip! Chop!"

"Oh, leave her be," spoke Grandma Alice teetering in. "The child must be simply exhausted!"

Grandma Alice's gaze matched Mary Ann's, much the same as the Nothing Fool's had before their final waltz together. In fact, Mary Ann noted with curiosity, come to think of it... She was standing in precisely the same spot as the Nothing Fool had been when she first spotted him from inside the Looking-Glass Globe. (A most curious coincidence, indeed!)

"Oh Maemae Alice! I've had the most amazingly fantastic dream EVER! You wouldn't believe it... Absolutely and fantastically amazing!" Mary Ann squealed gleefully.

Grandma Alice sat down in the wooden rocking chair next to the bed and after thoughtful pause, quite comfortingly said, "Oh, wouldn't I?"

She brushed an amber strand of hair from her granddaughter's forehead and on the freckled spot directly between her eyes, planted a soft kiss. In doing so, she drew back suddenly, looking concerned.

"Have you a fever, my dear?" Grandma Alice asked, checking the child's temperature at her neck and palms. "How odd..." she continued coyly. "There seems to be only fever in your head. Why don't you give us a good cough. See if that does the trick," she finished with a wink.

So Mary Ann breathed deeply from her belly then coughed. And out from her mouth spat a short blast of fire with a fiercely-tipped dragonfly in tow, who sputtered to catch himself frailly in flight.

Unable to contain her excitement, she shrieked, "FEROCIOUS! You're... ALIVE!"

The dragonfly turned to her, nodding humbly, then chugged his wings for take-off on (presumably) a Journey of Great Importance.

Outside the window, sunny skies peeked on the horizon, past the pouring thunderclouds. Bridging the border of the town, a rainbow arched an invisible wall of spectacular color spectrum.

119

Mary Ann felt a tug at her heart, then closed her eyes and jumped on the back of the ferociously magical dragonfly to the Rainbow of Hope.

Flying free, they swooped out the window, dodging each and every raindrop. Eeping in to her right, Professor Firefly tipped a quite smart-looking hat.

"Got yourself a light shade?!" Mary Ann called to him, with an unstoppable smile splattered ear to ear.

"And it looks like you've got yourself something too!" called the Good Witch on her new flying vacuum cleaner (having replaced the decrepit broom), zooming to the left. From beneath her witch's hat, she produced a pen of platinumest gold which she kissed for effect. The pen floated light as a feather through the clearing skies straight into Mary Ann's hand.

Mary Ann took the pen in hand and raised it proudly high as if about to paint with words the very path ahead. Onwards toward the bright horizon she cried victoriously, "To ADVENTURE!"

THE NEVER-END

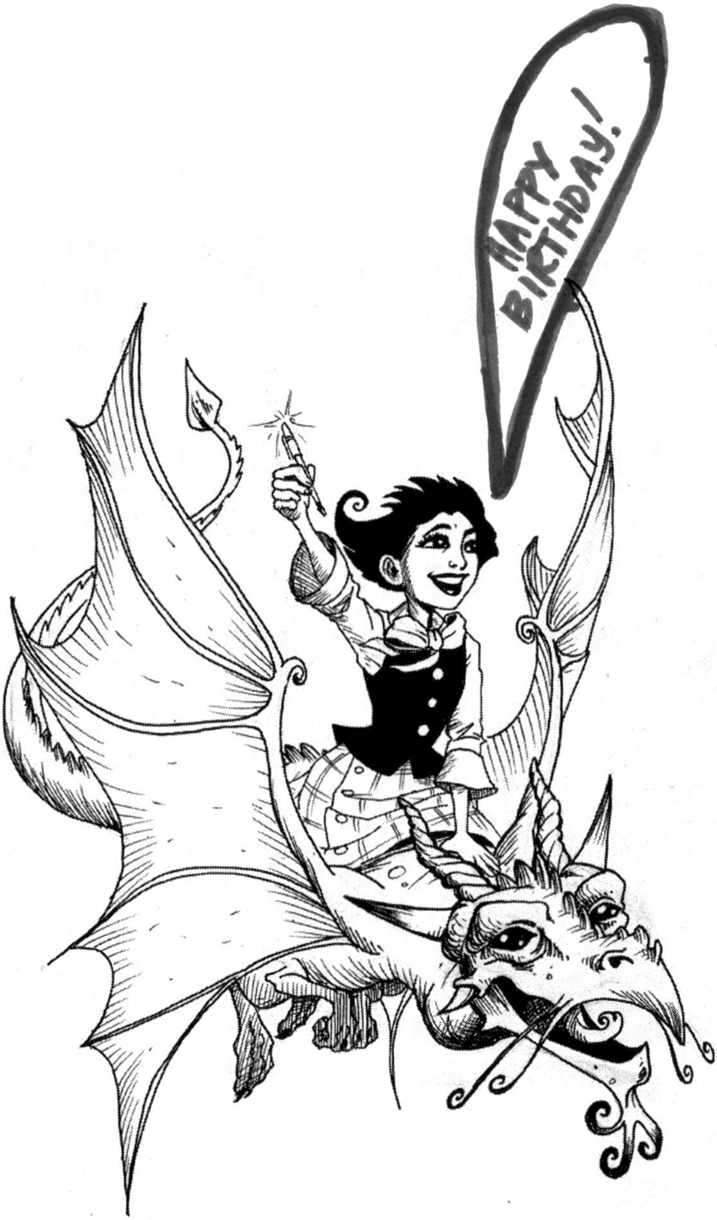
HAPPY BIRTHDAY!